SNOOKER
TODAY

WORLD
SNOOKER
EMBASSY WORLD S

SNOOKER
TODAY

Peter Arnold

WHSMITH
EXCLUSIVE
· BOOKS ·

Photographic Acknowledgements
All photographs reproduced in this book were supplied
by David Muscroft Photography

This edition produced exclusively for
W H Smith

Published by
The Hamlyn Publishing Group Limited
Bridge House, London Road, Twickenham, Middlesex TW1 3SB

ISBN 0 600 55235 7

Printed in Hong Kong by Mandarin Offset

CONTENTS

The Growth of the Game

Dennis Taylor relieves the tension of a match lasting two days and ending past midnight with a gesture of triumph. Referee John Williams looks as if he can hardly believe the World Championship of 1985 is over.

It was 12.23 am on Monday morning, 29 April 1985, a time when most people are normally fast asleep, the alarm clock set for the beginning of another week at work. A tall, elegant Englishman with striking auburn hair was just coming to the end of his fortnight's work at the Crucible Theatre, Sheffield. He was preparing to cut the final black into the top pocket to become world snooker champion for the third year running. It was not a notably difficult shot – he would get it nine times in ten. But he missed.

At that moment, eighteen and a half million televiewers all over Britain gasped, hid their heads in their hands, shouted encouragement for his rival, or just reached for another sip of cocoa, depending on temperament and who they were supporting. A minute or so later the other player, a convivial Irishman with a comfortable waistline and large futuristic spectacles, sank the black, wagged his finger and, holding his cue at each end, raised it horizontally above his head in a gesture of triumph at becoming world champion after 13 years of trying. The nation went happy and exhausted to bed, and next morning discussed the outcome of the latest manifestation of civilized gladiatorial combat. The audience was a record for BBC2, and the biggest-ever British audience for any television programme after midnight.

The game of snooker had reached a new peak on a popularity graph which had shown a rapid upward trend since 1969, when BBC2 had begun its series *Pot Black*. The man who missed the black in that 1985 final, Steve Davis, was already the richest sportsman in the country. The man who finally won the match, Dennis Taylor, was to receive unprecedented adulation when he returned to his home in Coalisland, County Tyrone.

But it had not always been like this. The official championship had not been held for a decade or so throughout the 1950s and 1960s, after a dispute between the professionals and the ruling body. There were, however, unofficial Professional Match-Play Championships, but the champion, Fred Davis, decided that it was not worth defending in 1957, so small was public interest.

To discover the origins of the game which has become such a crowd-pleaser in today's technological age, we must go back a few hundred years to its ancestor, billiards. However, we do not have to go as far back as the pre-Christian era, as Shakespeare would have us believe when, in *Antony and Cleopatra*, he had the Egyptian queen invite her attendant Charmian to a game with 'Let's to billiards' (Charmian pleaded a sore arm).

Billiards was adapted from an outdoor game which, instead of using pockets or holes, employed an arch and a pin (which the players tried to hit). The balls were propelled with maces (sticks which were curved and flattened at one end). Although this game was popular in France, their Church frowned on it as a waste of good men's time. Incidentally, football in England faced the same trouble, being banned by Parliament so that yeomen could get on with the more profitable archery practice.

Louis XI (1461–83) brought the game indoors to play it with more privacy, so

Steve Davis can still raise a smile after losing the 1985 World Championship in the most agonising way possible, on the very last black after being eight frames up.

The billiards room at Bartley's, in Bath, where 180 years ago the mysteries of side were discovered and John Carr sold the gullible public his magic 'twisting chalk'.

creating the first billiards table. Apart from this, the game was much the same as the outdoor variety, with the table having an arch at one end (near where the black spot is today) and a pin at the other (near the brown spot). (Louis was the first of several monarchs to be connected with the game. One hundred years later Mary Queen of Scots had a more dubious association, for after she was beheaded in 1587 her corpse was wrapped in the cloth of her own billards table.)

The change into billiards as it is played now came gradually. The cloth, originally green to simulate grass, was perfected by companies in the West of England (West of England cloth is still used on the tables in the major snooker tournaments). 'Pockets', when they were introduced, were originally wooden boxes (called hazards), which were later replaced by nets. The balls were initially made of wood, but soon after 1800 began to be made of ivory, which gave the game the satisfying aesthetic click, as ball hit ball. Since ivory was expensive (not all elephant tusks were suitable), composition balls were widely used, and around 1870, when 'celluloid' was invented, the makers turned to synthetic plastic. Improvements in the material have led to today's Super Crystalate balls.

Originally each player had a ball and these were the only two used, the third ball being introduced in the second half of the 18th century. This ball was called a carom, and scoring consisted in winning hazards (the potting of a ball) and caroms (now called cannons). From the 1730s on cues were used in addition to maces. At first the 'wrong' end, or tail, of the mace was used (*queue* is French for tail) for shots when the ball was against the rail. But by the end of the century the spatulate end of the mace had ceased to be used at all, and the cue had taken over.

Leather tips were invented in 1807 by a French infantry officer called Mingaud, while he was serving a prison sentence for debt. On his release he became a good player with the help of his tip, and discovered that by holding the cue vertically above the ball, and hitting downwards to slice against the side of it, he could make the ball swerve violently. The mace had been held more or less upright, with the curved end striking the ball; and the shot is still known by the French word for the mace – *massé*.

Remarkably quickly after the invention of the tip the enterprising John Carr – who was a marker (scorer) in billiards rooms (owned by John Bartley) at Bath – discovered that the tips were useful for imparting side spin to make the balls rebound at odd angles from the cushion. Bartley was very proficient at this, particularly since he screwed his tip into the ceiling before a shot to give better contact with the ball. Later, Carr began to market chalk for this very purpose. He called it 'twisting chalk', but it was, of course, common chalk which he sold at inflated prices for its 'special' qualities.

Other developments included the introduction of the cushion to replace the rails, which were originally used to keep the balls on the tables. The cushions were at first made with flock or down, but became much more efficient when rubber was introduced in 1835. Ten years later the new vulcanized rubber made the cushions the vital part of the table they remain to this day. (To maintain billiards' royal connections, an early set of these cushions was given to Queen Victoria, who had had a table erected at Windsor a few years earlier.) By now the bed of the table, originally oak but sometimes expensive marble, had become slate. The equipment and game was now very recognizably billiards as it is played today.

Although the first champions to make their names on a billiards table did not play snooker at all (which came a little later), they did develop many of the skills which the snooker players of today practise. Edwin (known as Jonathon) Kentfield of Brighton was the first generally accepted champion, around 1820. He resisted a challenge from John Carr, the inventor of 'magic' chalk, but relinquished the title in 1849 when declining to accept a challenge from John Roberts senior, of Liverpool.

Roberts lost the championship to William Cook in 1870, at St. James's Hall in London. The match lasted just over five hours before a capacity crowd of a few hundred, which included the Prince of Wales. Tickets changed hands for £5 each, an enormous sum in those days. Cook soon lost the title to Roberts' son,

John Thurston's original billiards hall at Catherine Street, London in 1839. The later, more famous, Thurston's was in Leicester Square until bombed in the Second World War.

John Roberts junior, who was to have a big part to play in the spread of the new game of snooker.

While billiards enjoyed a boom, the championship was formalized, the Billiards Association was founded (in 1885) and rules were drawn up. One of the first great players was John Roberts junior – the 19th-century equivalent of Joe Davis – who was so far ahead of his contemporaries that he could ignore the championship, and earn more money and fame by occasionally challenging the 'official' champion, giving him a start and beating him. He went off on frequent trips around the world, particularly to India, where he opened a factory to make tables and was engaged as court billiards player, at a large salary, by the Maharajah of Jaipur. And it was here in India that snooker itself was invented. The main credit for that goes to a young army officer, subaltern Sir Neville Chamberlain of the Devonshire Regiment.

Meanwhile, other games, apart from billiards, were being played on billiards tables, usually in order to involve more than two players or to introduce interesting gambling elements. Popular in the officers' mess at Jubbulpore, where Chamberlain was stationed, was a game called Life Pool. Each player had a cue ball of a different colour, and each player's object ball was the cue ball of the previous player. The player with the yellow ball tried to pot the green, the green player the pink, the pink player the red, and so on. When a player's ball was potted, he lost a life, and when he'd lost three lives, he retired. Eventually only two players were left each trying to pot the other's ball, and the winner took all the stakes.

An interesting addition to this game was a 'floating' black ball. When a player potted his specified object ball, he had the opportunity to pot the black, and if successful would be paid an additional stake by all the other players. This game was called Black Pool, and has similarities to the 'eight-ball' game of Pool played today, in that the black is the ball which has to be potted last to win the game, after the opponent's balls have been potted.

Another game which contributed to snooker was called Pyramids. It was played with 15 reds placed in the familiar triangle, with the ball at the apex of the triangle placed on what is now usually called the pink spot, but was then called the 'pyramid spot', and in fact still is in the official rules of snooker, although of course it is occupied now by the pink ball and not the tip of the pyramid. In Pyramids the players attempted to pot the reds, and for each red potted a player received a stake from his opponents.

It was Chamberlain who had the inspiration of combining Black Pool with Pyramids, so that 15 reds, the black, and some of the colours were on the table at the same time. Potting a red entitled a player to pot one of the coloured balls for an extra stake. The main differences were that Chamberlain did not have the blue or brown balls, which were added later; there was still no breakbuilding; and the coloured balls were still of equal value, so the game did not yet have the subtleties of the current game. But what made the game played by Chamberlain a landmark in the development of snooker was that he invented the name.

In 1875 a subaltern arrived at Jubbulpore fresh from the Royal Military Academy at Woolwich. He informed the company that a first-year cadet at Woolwich was referred to as a 'snooker', this being a corruption of the French word *neux*, meaning a new man. The term was derisory, and implied that the 'snooker' was still wet behind the ears. Chamberlain later recalled how, soon after he'd been told of this expression of disdain, one of his party missed a simple pot of a colour into a corner pocket, and Chamberlain called him 'a regular snooker'. He then had to explain what he meant, but smoothed over any ill-feeling by explaining that at this new game everybody was a 'snooker', and that this, in fact, sounded like a good name for the game. This was agreed, and snooker came into being. When Chamberlain moved on to the Central India Horse regiment, he introduced the game to the hill station at Ootacamund, known as the Ooty Club, where he spent the summer. For the first time the rules were written down, and hung on the wall of the billiards room.

One evening in Calcutta, in 1885, Roberts junior and Chamberlain were

Tom Newman (left), who was in every World Billiards Championship final in the 1920s and won the title six times, with Sydney Lee, an amateur champion of the 1930s.

dining with the Maharajah of Cooch Behar. News of the new game had already reached England through army officers on leave, and Roberts now learned from Chamberlain the rules. He brought them home, and since he also visited Australia, New Zealand, South Africa and America, he was the best possible man to spread the gospel. Three of those countries became prominent in the game. However, America still prefers pool, and strangely India, where it started, has been one of the slowest countries to switch allegiance from billiards to snooker.

Nowhere did snooker immediately supplant billiards although, looking back, it is difficult to see why it did not. The reason was more probably the cost of the complete set of balls than a preference for billiards as a game.

From the turn of the century the World Billiards Championship was held, if not every year, then very regularly up to 1934, when interest finally petered out. The champions in this era were the great names of the game – the Britishers Charles Dawson, H.W. Stephenson, Melbourne Inman, Willie Smith, Tom Newman (of the extraordinarily long jaw) and Joe Davis, and Walter Lindrum, of Australia. To these names might be added Tom Reece (Britain), six times runner-up, and Clark McConachy of New Zealand, who lost to Joe Davis in the 1932 final, won the title in 1951 when there was an attempt to revive interest, and lost it to Rex Williams in 1968, when there was a second revival, which still continues, although without threatening the popularity of snooker.

One big drawback of billiards was the frequent tinkering with the rules to prevent huge breaks. One of the biggest had been made by Tom Reece in 1907, when he scored 499,135 unfinished, by means

of an anchor cannon, in which all three balls are grouped in the jaws of a corner pocket. His break lasted for about five weeks, at which point the hall was wanted for another match with Reece's opponent long since having gone home! What point there could have been in watching, counting, or even making such a break, it is difficult to imagine.

Of those pre-Second World War billiards champions only one, Joe Davis, was born after 1900, and he was the one who spotted the potential of snooker. At that time the game was suffering growing pains. Although there had been British Amateur Championships since 1916 they were of such poor quality that the 1918 championship had been won by an American after just a few weeks practice. The following year the Billiards Association and Billiards Control Club amalgamated and standardized the game's rules. However, the request by a Nottinghamshire player and billiards hall owner, Tom Dennis, for the governing body to organize a professional championship was declined because it thought that there was insufficient popular interest. Fortunately, a Midlands promoter Bill Camkin then approached Joe Davis, who persuaded the BACC to promote a professional snooker championship. The first tournament of what is now regarded as the World Professional Championship took place in 1927, when Davis beat Tom Dennis in the Birmingham final. Davis' consecutive breaks of 32, 34, and 35, then considered quite remarkable, helped earn him prize money of £6.10s.

Davis was primarily a billiards player, but he promoted snooker whenever he could, and from 1928 to 1932 was World Champion at both games. However, in 1933 he lost his billiards title to the Australian Walter Lindrum, who was probably the best billiards player of all time, and failed to regain it in Melbourne in 1934. With Lindrum in Australia there were no more World Billiards Championships until he relinquished the title in 1950.

Snooker, meanwhile, held its World Championship every year, and Davis kept winning, beating off usually no more than four or five challengers each year. The game finally overtook billiards in 1936. Horace Lindrum, the 23-year-old nephew of Walter, came from Australia to challenge, and in his first frame in England made a break of 71. He reached the final, and led Davis in the 61-frame match at several stages, his best being 27-24 on the final day. But Davis came back to take the last ten frames for a winning margin of 34-27. This exciting match confirmed snooker as a spectacle which people would pay to watch.

The big championships before the Second World War were held at Thurston's, Leicester Square, London, where Joe Davis was unbeatable. His final challenger for the world title in 1940 was his 12-years-younger brother, Fred, whom he beat 37-35.

After the war, Fred lost in the 1946 semi-final to Horace Lindrum, who played Joe in a 145-frame final lasting a fortnight. Joe twice beat the championship record break, with 133 and 136, on

Opposite: The first, and still the greatest, name in snooker is that of Joe Davis, the first World Champion, who retired from the championship unbeaten after 20 years.

Walter Lindrum (left) and Joe Davis, great rivals at billiards. Davis was World Champion four times up to 1932, but Lindrum beat him in the finals of 1933 and 1934. The greatest billiards player in the world, Lindrum left the snooker scene to Davis.

his way to beating Lindrum 78-67. The two finalists earned £1,500 each, which was then big money, after which Joe retired from the World Championship to give others a chance. He had been champion for 20 years, and had never been beaten on level terms.

Joe then became chairman of the Professional Billiards Players Association, and joint promoter with Sydney Smith at the Leicester Square Hall, which opened on the site of the Old Thurston's, which had been bombed in the war. Joe was Mr. Snooker, dealing with the early post-war BBC television experiments (usually exhibitions, or more or less arranged matches).

Joe Davis' act of giving up the world title had not really been a sacrifice, since he proceeded to emulate John Roberts, and challenged and beat succeeding champions. But if he expected his brother to succeed him as champion, he was initially disappointed. The 1947 World Championship was won, rather surprisingly, by Walter Donaldson, a single-minded Scot, who not only beat Lindrum in the semi-final, but Fred Davis 82-63 in the final. Later, Joe Davis took his revenge by beating Donaldson 49-42 in a challenge match, while brother Fred took the title in 1948 by 84-61.

In 1949 Fred Davis inflicted his first defeat at level terms on his brother Joe in a humorous fashion. It was in a sealed handicap match sponsored by the *Sunday Empire News*, for which Fred wrote. The idea was that the two played on level terms over 71 frames, at the end of which an envelope would be opened to reveal the handicap. Fred won 36-35, but when the envelope was opened it was discovered that he had to give two frames to his previously unbeaten opponent, and so lost on handicap! It appeared that the sports editor of the newspaper, in settling the handicap, had been unable to admit that his contributor was not the better player. Fred beat Joe twice more on level terms in the remainder of their careers.

Joe Davis' gesture in relinquishing his crown did not bring the expected further interest in snooker, and after the immediate post-war days, when most sports

Horace Lindrum was Walter Lindrum's nephew, and a great player at both billiards and snooker. He was Joe Davis' strongest challenger for the World Snooker Championship before and after the Second World War, and won it in 1952 when the British professionals did not take part.

Rex Williams (left) and Fred Davis. Davis was the world's leading snooker player from the late 1940s, and throughout the 1950s, while Williams was the player who did most to revive the World Championship after the apathy of the 1950s.

boomed, there was a slump. Despite the sponsorship deals of the *News of the World* and the *Sporting Record* newspapers, the crowds dwindled. The professional set-up was too much of a closed shop, though Joe Davis did his best to revive the game by visiting Canada, where he beat their champion, George Chenier (who used a two-piece cue way back in the 1940s). Joe invited Chenier to England where, in 1950, the Canadian made a break of 144, which should have been a new record. However, the authorities were so anxious to keep the record in Britain that they did not recognize it until after Joe Davis, playing Chenier, had made 146 at Houldsworth Hall, Manchester, five weeks later, whereupon they allowed Chenier's previous effort. The Canadian told the authorities what he thought of them and returned to Canada, where he was also a great pool player.

The year 1950 was also enlivened by an argument between the BACC and the PBPA, when the latter wanted to introduce a rule whereby a player making a foul stroke could be asked by his opponent to play again. While this rule is now an essential part of the game, it was then refused. Two years later, after another dispute, this time over terms and conditions with the BACC, no British professionals entered the World Championship – the two finalists were the only entrants, the eventual winner Horace Lindrum, of Australia, and Clark McConachy, of New Zealand. Instead, the British professionals organized Professional Match-Play Championships, and in some reference books these have latterly become accepted as continuations of the World Championships, with Lindrum's title 'written out' of history. But, with Fred Davis winning each year to 1956, even these ceased in 1957 due to lack of public interest. Fred had had enough by this time, and did not enter, with John Pulman beating Jackie Rea in the 1957 final.

The Leicester Square Hall had closed in 1955, but, before it did so, Joe Davis made the first maximum 147 break in approved match conditions. Snooker then went into a rapid decline, there being only six active professionals (including Joe Davis, who entered his sixtieth year in 1961). Eventually Rex Williams revived the players' association and the World Championship, which resumed in 1964 in a new format, with the champion Pulman accepting individual challenges for his crown. During the next five years he made seven successful defences.

In 1968 the PBPA was reformed as the World Professional Billiards and Snooker Association, and became the professional governing body. Three new professionals were admitted to the fold – the first since 1951. They were Ray Reardon, John Spencer and Gary Owen. All took part in an eight-man tournament for the World Championship in

Alex Higgins, with tie, before he became World Champion in 1972. Higgins' exciting play brought new life to snooker as a spectator sport and contributed to the current boom.

1969, with Spencer beating Owen in the final.

At about the same time television took a hand in snooker's fortunes. The second BBC channel had opened in 1969 and now decided to show minority sports, preferably those which were colourful and cheap to televise. Snooker recommended itself as an ideal subject and on 23 July 1969 *Pot Black* was launched. It was not the first time snooker had been screened, but it was the most successful showing, and reached a new public. The players became known, their exhibition fees and bookings increased, sponsors appeared (Players No. 6 cigarettes sponsored the 1969 World Championship and Park Drive, of rival company Gallaher, quickly followed), snooker halls improved, and new venues were built.

In 1970 the World Championship was held twice, once in England and once in Australia, where there were entries from the Australian-based players – Eddie Charlton, Norman Squire, Warren Simpson and Paddy Morgan, and Perrie Mans from South Africa. Reardon won the first title and Spencer the second.

A big fillip to the game came with the 1972 championships, when there was no sponsor, but 16 contestants, eight of whom had to qualify for the first round of the competition proper. One of the qualifiers was a 22-year-old Irishman, Alex Higgins, whose image was quite unlike that of the other professionals. He was untidy, did not hide the fact that he gambled and drank, and attracted plenty of girls. Higgins beat Spencer in the final, and in so doing put an end to the era of the two Davises and Pulman.

Although this was the biggest upset in the history of snooker, it gained scant attention from the newspapers. After all, the final had been held in the British Legion club at Selly Oak, Birmingham. Conditions were primitive in the extreme, with spectators sitting on beer crates and, more often than not, having to leave the building if they needed the toilets. (It was a long way from St. James's Hall, and the Prince of Wales watching the billiards championship 102 years before.) With prize money of just £800, with £480 going to Alex, small wonder the press took very little notice.

Gradually, however, Alex became good copy. His demeanour was a mixture of Wild West gun-slinger, toreador and prize-fighter. He lived for snooker, was hyper-active and the fans loved him. Best of all, he played with an urgency unknown to the old professionals. In the days of Fred Davis and Pulman, a player might wander from the scene while his opponent was making a break, summoned back by a bell. Higgins was the complete opposite, utterly wrapped up in the game, anxiously chain-smoking and looking on when he was not at the table. And when he did get his chance he played his shots with such speed and flair that he became known as 'Hurricane' Higgins.

The traditionalists were scandalized, and predicted that such a man would burn himself out in no time. But it was burning of a different kind which threatened to stop snooker's progress.

Television was proving a marvellous medium for spreading the sport. In 1973 the World Championship was sponsored by Park Drive cigarettes, and television showed some of a semi-final and final. The championship was streamlined into a fortnight at one venue, the City Exhibition Halls, Manchester, and during the two weeks was watched by 25,000 spectators. Higgins lost a semi-final to Eddie Charlton, and Reardon regained the title 38-32.

But while television helped make the game immensely popular, it also brought problems. The intense lighting needed for colour broadcasts made the rails of the table hot, and in a previous Park Drive event had made the plastic facing on the rails begin to curl. Worse, when the lights were switched on for transmitting the 1973 final, Reardon, who was leading 27-25, immediately lost three frames and complained that he could not see. The floodlights on the crowd were then switched off, enabling Reardon to pull himself together in time to win.

Lighting for television continued to be a problem until 1976, when Nick Hunter, the BBC producer most associated with snooker broadcasts, brought the lighting engineers and the players together to sort out an acceptable and efficient method of lighting. But the lighting problem has not entirely gone away, for as recently as 1987 Higgins complained of auditorium lighting in the Benson and Hedges

The first year at the Crucible Theatre, Sheffield, and the second year of Embassy sponsorship, saw an old champion John Spencer, whose first World Championship had been won eight years before, win his last world title in 1977.

Masters at Wembley, causing play to be briefly interrupted.

Although Norwich Union, an insurance company, had entered the sponsorship field, Park Drive had withdrawn from the World Championship in 1975, and the championship was switched to Australia for a second time, being awarded to Eddie Charlton Promotions. The prize money was a healthy £18,900 and Eddie nearly won the largest part of it himself. In a final which was the best of 61 frames, he led 29-23, before Reardon ran off seven consecutive frames, eventually winning 31-30. Reardon now took over from Spencer (who had been the leading player of the late 1960s and early 1970s) to dominate snooker until 1979.

In 1976, the championship found new sponsors in Embassy, the Wills brand of cigarettes, which still sponsors it. There were two venues, Middlesbrough Town Hall for one half of the draw, and Wythenshawe Forum for the other and the final. This championship, organized by a company called 'Q' Promotions (which soon afterwards folded up) was beset by problems. The Middlesbrough venue was inadequate, and one table at Wythenshawe was discovered by Eddie Charlton to have oversized pockets. The final itself began with bad temper. Reardon, who had come through the Middlesbrough half of the draw, complained about the running of the table and the television lighting, which had been installed for the final, and which put a dazzling reflection on the balls. The lights had to be rehung in a more acceptable manner, and producer Nick Hunter was provoked into getting together his consortium of experts to ensure that there was no more trouble.

Reardon's opponent in the final was a revived Higgins who, with his army of supporters urging him on, had won three very close matches, 15-14 against Thorburn and then Spencer, and 20-18 against Charlton. Conditions were gradually improved during the intervals of the final, and Reardon, after being behind more than once, eventually won fairly easily at 27-16.

The 1977 championship was a big step forward. A new promoter, Mike Watterson, saw the possibilities of a new venue, the Crucible Theatre at Sheffield, and Embassy, after the previous year's disasters, were persuaded to continue their sponsorship. It was the right decision for the game and the sponsors.

The championship ran smoothly, the television coverage was increased and was good, there were 24 entrants and new names came to the fore, particularly Cliff Thorburn of Canada, who became the first Canadian to reach the final. But it was an old favourite, John Spencer, with a new two-piece cue, who won the title, coming back from 15-11 down to begin the last day at 18-18, and eventually winning 25-21. It had been inevitable from before the final that the winner would be the first person in history to take the World Championship using a two-piece cue. Thorburn, like most Canadians, had used one for a long time, while Spencer had picked one up on a visit to Canada and had begun to use it only a few weeks earlier.

This championship proved a happy co-operation between snooker and television. Meanwhile, the weekly series *Pot Black* was increasing its audience, as more and more found this attractive spot on the otherwise very much minority channel, BBC2. The players for *Pot Black* were selected by commentator Ted Lowe, the 'Voice of Snooker', who had managed the Leicester Square Hall for Joe Davis and Sydney Smith. He also chose the players for the Pontins Professional Championship, for which he was consultant. Pontins, the holiday camp chain, had run a Festival of Snooker, lasting one week, at their Prestatyn camp since 1974. There was an invited professional event and an open event, which professionals and amateurs alike could enter.

Higgins, after threatening to walk out of *Pot Black* in 1972 half-way through the series, was not invited again for some years, and was also rejected by the Pontins Festival. However, in 1977 he entered the open tournament and won, beating Terry Griffiths, then an amateur, by 7-4 in the final, even though Griffiths had received three blacks start in each frame.

That year, Warners, another holiday camp chain, joined the snooker circuit with an open event at Sinah Warren, while Mike Watterson promoted a United Kingdom Professional Championship, sponsored by the makers of Super Crystalate balls. Three relatively new names made it to the semi-finals at the Blackpool Tower Circus to join Higgins: Welshman Doug Mountjoy, Englishman John Virgo and Irishman Patsy Fagan. Fagan beat Mountjoy 12-9 in the final. Alas, by 1987 he had not reached another major final.

This tournament sparked two controversies over the 'deliberate miss' rule. In the final frame of a match between Rex Williams and Willie Thorne, Williams felt that Thorne was guilty of such a miss, and gained a big advantage when the referee failed to call it. Thorne went on to win the frame and match, and Williams angrily went home. Later, when Thorne was allegedly overheard admitting that the miss had been deliberate, the promoter, the WPBSA secretary and referee John Williams disqualified him and reinstated Rex Williams. (Rex, at the time, was no longer chairman of the WPBSA, having resigned six months earlier because he did not think that he was getting enough support from fellow members.)

Perrie Mans in play in the 1978 World Championship final, but it was the old maestro Ray Reardon who won, his sixth and last title.

Perhaps this episode confirmed a lack of judgement in the Association because Thorne complained on hearing of this improperly made decision by only two members and a quorum reinstated him, just in time to tell Williams, who had been summoned to return, as he arrived back at the arena. It was an unfortunate episode.

The second problem occurred in the final itself, when Mountjoy was adjudged to have made a deliberate miss, and was considerably upset by the decision. These decisions are very difficult to make, of course, because a player is entitled to try to graze the side of the object ball – he does not have to hit it dead centre.

Wembley staged its first snooker tournament in 1977 when the boxing promoter, Mike Barrett, staged the Dry Blackthorn Cup at the Conference Centre. Fagan won it before London Weekend television cameras, but the event did not last. The following year Embassy and the Crucible Theatre looked to capitalize on the growing snooker boom, when there were 28 entries for the World Championship, and prize money increased to £24,000, of which £7,500 was reserved for the winner. The quarter-finals featured two Englishmen, Graham Miles and Fred Davis, two Canadians, Cliff Thorburn and Bill Werbeniuk, a Welshman, Ray Reardon, an Irishman, Patsy Fagan, an Australian, Eddie Charlton, and a South African, Perrie Mans. Reardon won his sixth and last title by beating Mans 25-18 in the final.

Forward Chemicals, Holsten Lager, Tolly Cobbold, and Coral Racing were the new sponsors on the circuit in 1978-79, joining Benson and Hedges (who still sponsored the Masters, and who now moved to their present venue at the Wembley Conference Centre) and Embassy, who retained the World Professional Snooker Championship. Coral sponsored the UK Professional (Super Crystalate pulled out, having been disappointed by the December crowds at Blackpool). This tournament, too, found an impressive new venue at the Guild Hall, Preston, where it remains. Doug Mountjoy beat David Taylor in the final to make up for his disappointment the year before. The Pontins Open had a final which, in retrospect, looks very interesting. A youngster called Steve Davis gave the 16-year-old Jimmy White 30 points per frame, but still won 7-3.

The 1979 World Championship was the one at which the nation as a whole became aware of snooker. BBC2 doubled its coverage from 1978, when there had been 50-minute highlights every day, some live transmissions (including BBC1's *Grandstand*), and live coverage of the final. Since the seven million audience at the end of the 1978 final had been twice that for *Pot Black*, the BBC now decided to expand its coverage to take in many more live transmissions. They were lucky. By the middle Saturday all the previous world champions were out, and a new hero was waiting to be crowned – he turned out to be one the public approved of wholeheartedly.

Terry Griffiths was the man. (Since this was his first year as a professional he had to qualify for the final stages of the tournament.) In the Coral UK Championship six months earlier, he had led Rex Williams 8-2 in a preliminary round, only to lose 9-8. To the general public he was unknown. Then came what was the big highlight of the World Championship, Griffiths' quarter-final with Alex Higgins. It was a match of superb play throughout, with Higgins starting so brilliantly that he made centuries in the second and third frames to lead 6-2. From 8-8, when the third session started, neither player could get more than one in front. Then came the final frame, with Griffiths making a 107 break to go forward.

The television audience found this cliff-hanger magnificent entertainment. When Griffiths' semi-final with Charlton produced another match of drama, but of a different kind, with Charlton waging a war of attrition and Griffiths surviving it to win 19-17 from 17-16 down, they stayed with it to the end, even though this was not until 1.40 am in the morning. The last session had lasted 5 hours 25 minutes for just eight frames. Once again Griffiths won with a big break, 97, after trailing 48-0.

The personable Welshman was interviewed by David Vine after the match. In an atmosphere of tired euphoria there was little of the minute analysis of such-and-such an important shot. 'I'm in the final now, you know,' said a beaming Terry, as if he were still an amateur enjoying a game with the big boys. And the nation wished him well.

The final was against an Irishman, Dennis Taylor, who at the time was a 'nearly man', a spear-carrier who did not quite know how to win. He was to have his day seven years later, and to enjoy as much popularity as anybody in the game. But in 1979 the new television fans wanted only one winner, and they got him, rather comfortably in the end – 24-16 – although it had been 15-15 after two days, with Taylor leading at 11-9 and 14-12. On the last day Griffiths seemed to shed the tiredness gained from his previous two long matches, playing as well as ever to take the last seven frames.

Griffiths, who had been a milkman and a door-to-door insurance collector, became, through television, an overnight hero, and was soon earning money he had hardly dared dream of a few weeks earlier. As for the television public, who had watched the antics and agony of Higgins, the determination and despondency of Charlton, the gameness and gallantry of Griffiths, they decided that they could not have too much of this exciting new human-drama-cum-soap-opera of modern snooker.

Truly the start of a new era. An unknown had battled through to be World Champion and the television public had been hooked by the drama. Terry Griffiths with the trophy in 1979.

THE PROFESSIONAL GAME TODAY

Among the reports on Griffiths' great victory in 1979 – 'Old Order Changes', and 'Terry Griffiths: People's Champion' – *Snooker Scene*, the leading snooker journal, carried a few paragraphs about the nine-hour annual general meeting of the World Professional Billiards and Snooker Association, held on the day following the championships.

One topic of discussion was who would be exempt from qualifying for the 1980 World Championships at the Crucible. Previously, the first eight men in the rankings (then based entirely on the results of the three previous World Championships) had gone straight on to the final 16-man tournament. But since every player now had a vote, and there were more than 16 professionals, it was not surprising that this system was outvoted. The lesser players wanted more places available for the small fry. The system they approved was that only the two finalists would be excused from qualifying, in this instance Terry Griffiths and Dennis Taylor. Even Ray Reardon, the No. 1 in the rankings, would have to qualify.

There was an immediate reaction from the leading players who formed a new body, the Professional Snooker Association Ltd., which became a pressure group and a potential rival to the governing body. Its first success was to enforce the scrapping of the new exemption system. There were to be 24 places at the Crucible, not 16, and 16 of those places would be reserved for the first 16 in the rankings; eight were left for qualifiers.

Since there were many members who belonged to both the WPBSA and the PSA, the meetings of the two bodies were generally held one after the other. And the PSA managed to get the WPBSA to adopt a compromise voting arrangement. While all professionals would be members of the WPBSA, only those ranked (21 players in 1979) would be allowed votes, and the top ten would form the committee. This was later modified as the rankings were extended, and voting rights were given to all players who had featured in the top 20, plus elected officers. The committee could include non-players, provided the players stayed in the majority. The PSA was then wound up, and the WPBSA was reformed as a limited company.

One of the complaints of the leading players, as snooker became a major television event, was that not enough of the money now beginning to flood into the game was finding its way to them. It became the WPBSA's role to promote the major tournaments and negotiate the television and sponsorship contracts. Del Simmons and his International Snooker Agency became the contracts negotiator.

This episode has been symptomatic of the snooker of the 1980s. A sport which had become almost moribund was now changing into big business, and the players were not ideally equipped to handle it. Sponsors, promoters, and agents were appearing. The manoeuvring for position in the committees and board rooms sometimes matched that on the table.

Griffiths, the new working-class hero, found he was much in demand in his year as champion. Suddenly everybody wanted him for exhibitions, personal appearances and company promotions, and like other champions since, his form suffered accordingly. He began the new season by losing 17-16 to Cliff Thorburn in the Canadian Open, but back in Birmingham helped Wales to win a new event convincingly. This was snooker's first World Cup, promoted by Mike Watterson to provide a new format for BBC coverage.

Griffiths suffered another one-frame defeat in a long match, when losing the final of the Coral UK to John Virgo 14-13. Virgo showed great strength of character to win. He had been 11-7 ahead before the last session, but arrived late for it and was fined two frames. His 11-9 lead slipped into a 13-12 deficit, before he took the last two frames.

Virgo has not since managed to win another major tournament, and is one of those players whose natural ability appears to be inhibited on the big occasion. The 'pressures' often mentioned by the snooker commentators had been apparent for all to see a few weeks earlier, when Patsy Fagan – who had won the UK Championship two years previously – had been seen in the World Cup to be quite unable to use the rest. He has since struggled to conquer this mental block, and was ranked No. 42 in 1986.

The independent television companies, alarmed at the high ratings the BBC were picking up with snooker, televised the Padmore/Super Crystalate International from the Gala Baths, West Bromwich, through ATV, and the Wilsons Classic, from Manchester, through Granada Television. So now trade interests and a brewery were sponsoring the tournaments, although the former were almost forced to come forward because of the lack of sponsors.

However, Independent Television did not cover itself with glory in its snooker broadcasts. The previous year, 1979, John Spencer had made what should have been the first 147 maximum break seen on television, when the Thames Television cameras were covering the Holsten Lager International from the Fulcrum Centre, Slough. However, since Spencer and Thorburn had arrived late for their match, the producers decided that the one camera crew on duty should take their tea break. Thus history was missed, much to the chagrin of the sponsor, Thames and Spencer.

Griffiths showed a return to form with a victory in the Benson and Hedges Masters, and arrived at the Crucible for the 1980 World Championship apparently in good form. But the motivation which often seems to desert modern World Champions on their return to Sheffield was certainly not with Terry. Maybe he was exhausted at the end of his busy year of fame. He had an up-and-coming qualifier, Steve Davis, as his first opponent, and was soon losing 7-0 and then 10-3. A great effort brought Griffiths seven frames running to level the scores at 10-10, but then an over-ambitious shot in the next frame, which he had almost won, lost him the game on the black, and he went out 13-10.

The best-represented country in the quarter-finals was Canada, with Jim Wych, Kirk Stevens and Cliff Thorburn, who went through to take the final from Higgins. Thorburn came from behind, overcoming an attack of nerves, to become what some claim to be the first overseas player to take the title (others say Lindrum, in 1952, deserves this honour). Higgins, who had lessened his chances of winning by deserting a new sober method for his old cavalier style when leading 9-5, called Thorburn a 'grinder', and the nickname stuck.

Cliff Thorburn of Canada was the first, and so far only, non-British player to win the World Championship in full-scale competition with all the best players in the world. He beat Alex Higgins in the 1980 final.

Tony Knowles caused the biggest upset in snooker till then when, as a player unknown to the general public, he beat the World Champion, Steve Davis, 10-1 in the first round at the Crucible in 1982.

Thorburn had a tricky year as champion, just as Griffiths had, although in Cliff's case it was not due to overwhelming demands on his time. The public, unfortunately for him, would have preferred the flamboyant Higgins as champion, and regarded Thorburn as a 'foreigner' to whom the title had been lent. The paradox was that the attraction of television snooker had been located in the smartness, dignity, and control of the bow-tied and waistcoated players, qualities which the immaculate and good-looking Thorburn had more than anybody else, whereas Higgins was the exception which proved the rule.

The 1981 semi-final of the Benson and Hedges Masters provided an example of Thorburn's frustrations. After leading 5-1, the World Champion lost 6-5 to Higgins, who was so weak after a morning spent vomiting that he almost fell asleep during the match but nevertheless, with the Wembley crowd roaring him on, kept coming to life to make inspired breaks which won five frames in a row, the last big break starting on a fluke.

This Masters tournament ended with nearly 2,500 spectators for the final session, a record. A new sponsor, Yamaha Organs, took over the British Gold Cup, which had been inaugurated the year before, in 1980 at the Derby Assembly Rooms. This tournament was the first to be networked by ITV, and its high audience ratings proved the great attraction of snooker to audiences of all channels. Steve Davis won the title, as he had the UK Championship, and when he soon after added the first English Championship, sponsored by John Courage, he became a firm favourite for the 1981 World Championship.

Davis beat Jimmy White, Alex Higgins and Terry Griffiths before meeting champion Cliff Thorburn in the semi-final. This match ended Thorburn's reign as World Champion in an unsatisfactory way. Davis was being groomed for stardom by Barry Hearn, his manager, who looked after every aspect of his snooker life, which, in fact, was becoming practically his whole life. The pair operated from a snooker complex at Romford, to which Thorburn was invited before the championship for an exhibition match. Davis won 6-0 in his own environment, so boosting his confidence for the encounter ahead.

When it mattered, however, Thorburn appeared to be the player with the confidence, completely mastering Davis in one session in which he took four consecutive frames to lead 8-6, with Davis visibly demoralized as he failed to pot a ball for about an hour.

In the next session, however, the Romford factor really came into its own. With a Union Jack draped over the balcony, Davis' fans noisily began urging him on. When Thorburn, 9-8 ahead and with a vital shot to go further in front, was three times distracted as he lined it up, he naturally thought that what has been called the 'Romford Mafia' was out to get him. He missed the shot, lost the frame, and seethed for the rest of the match. In the final frame of the session Davis made a break which included the blue, enough for a 12-10 lead, and with the pink still on the table offered a handshake. It was a small breach of snooker etiquette, and Thorburn, indicating that the frame was not yet over, declined. He addressed the cue ball, but did not play it and, conceding, shook Davis' hand. After the match he apologized in a television interview for his demonstration. But he did not win another frame. Davis claimed in his autobiography that Thorburn snapped, and the good-natured Canadian had certainly found it more difficult to concentrate after a section of the audience had played its part.

Davis went on to win the final by beating Doug Mountjoy 18-12, and many thought that he might begin a period of complete domination as the 1981-82 season progressed. It was not so much his wins as the manner of achieving them which impressed. Having proved to everybody during the Thorburn match that he was hard enough to beat anybody in the world, he went out to play almost like a robot in a string of wins.

The Jameson International was a new event at the beginning of the 1981–82 season, with a winners' prize of £20,000, equal at the time to that of the World Championship itself. Davis beat Dennis Taylor in the final 9-0. There followed a significant 9-0 defeat of Jimmy White who, at 19 years of age, had just become the youngest winner of a professional tournament – the Langs Supreme Scottish Masters, in which he had beaten Davis 6-5 in the semi-final before beating Cliff Thorburn 9-4 in the final. It was only his second big professional tournament, the previous year's 1981 World Championship being the first, when Davis had beaten him 10-8. After White had lost 1-5 to Rex Williams in the Jameson International, he beat Davis again, 11-9, in the final of the Northern Ireland Classic. His rapid potting style appealed to the fans, and his manner of play marked him as a potential great player. But in the Coral UK Championship he met and was destroyed 9-0 by Davis in the semi-final. The difference between this match and the two White had won was that this one was on television. To the millions of television spectators Davis emphasized that he was 'the man', and he confirmed his ice-cool ruthlessness with a 16-3 defeat of Terry Griffiths in the final.

The 1981 final was the first of five fought out by Griffiths and Davis. Griffiths won two, including the Lada Classic, but even this tournament was a triumph for Davis. Lada, the car manufacturers, had taken over the sponsorship of the event at Oldham which was previously the Wilsons Classic. Wilsons, a Liverpool brewing company, had withdrawn their sponsorship when the event was scheduled for wider ITV coverage than the Granada region, where they sold their beers, not feeling that the increased fee was worthwhile. But it certainly proved so for Lada when Steve Davis, in his first-round match with Spencer, made the first televised 147 maximum break. It was ironic that Davis' opponent, Spencer, had been the victim of the television crews' meal break three years before which meant that his 147 had gone unrecorded. The more fortunate Davis enjoyed maximum television and video exposure, as well as winning a Lada car as a bonus.

Davis made this break after returning from a round the world trip with his manager Barry Hearn, who lost no chance to cash in on the world title. But the constant travelling and exhibition matches were tiring Davis, and it was clear that he could not go on forever winning in his semi-prepared condition. When the crash came it was as surprising as it was decisive. Davis' first-round opponent in the World Championship was Tony Knowles, a qualifier from Bolton, who had been a professional for just two years. Knowles won the first four frames and, after Davis had won one, reeled off six more. His main task was to keep his nerve as his good, sound snooker notched up the points while the World Champion could not get going.

Another first-round defeat – of Terry Griffiths, 10-6 to Willie Thorne – gave visions of victory to many players whose initial hopes had not been too high. One such aspirant was Jimmy White, who completed a dismal two years for the world No. 1, Cliff Thorburn, by beating him 10-4 in the first round. Another was Alex Higgins, who saw a big chance to regain the crown ten years after his first victory. These two players met in the semi-finals, and produced a marvellous match.

White was the youngest World Championship semi-finalist, having beaten Kirk Stevens, the previous holder of this record, in the quarter-final. The eight frames in the first session lasted less than two hours as the two fastest players in the game entertained the audience. At first the frames went in batches: three for Higgins, to lead 4-1; seven for White to 8-4; then three for Higgins to leave White 8-7 ahead after the first day.

The second day, which saw a determined Higgins practising from 6 o'clock in the morning, was less fluctuating, with the biggest gap being in favour of White at 11-8, but by the end of the third session Higgins had come back to level the game at 11-11. Higgins kept level at 12-12 with an amazing fluke with the brown off six cushions, and then went ahead for the first time since White had caught him at 4-4. White then made a break of 70 to level at 13-13, and gave away just nine points over the next two frames.

Alex Higgins, the 1982 World Champion, ten years after his first win. He called his wife Lynn and baby Lauren into the spotlight to celebrate.

At 15-13, White needed one more frame for a place in the final. But Higgins took the next frame, after which came the most exciting break of the tournament. With White leading 59-0 in the 30th frame, Higgins went for everything as only he can: a long green off his first red was followed by a long black from near the yellow spot off his second, instead of the defensive roll-up behind a baulk colour. The break continued with a screw-back off two cushions from a blue into a baulk pocket, and a long red into a baulk pocket. Higgins needed the black to clear the table with a 69 break, so levelling the match, and, on a high, took the deciding frame with breaks of 59 and 37.

Higgins' final opponent was Ray Reardon, who had held the championship six times, and who was seeded fourth. Reardon led 5-2 as Higgins suffered a reaction from his inspiring semi-final, but Higgins got ahead at 8-7 and stayed ahead until, at 15-12, Reardon won three to level. But Ray missed shots in the next two frames, and Alex finished with a flourish at 18-15, making a 135 break.

Higgins was so overcome on winning the 1982 World Championship that he called for his wife and baby to join him in the television spotlight. It was a tearful scene, with Higgins afterwards proclaiming that he was the 'people's champion'.

Reardon's consolation was that he now became the world's top-ranked player, although his one-point advantage over Higgins was a result of the Irishman being docked two points (and fined £200) by the WPBSA in 1981, after misconduct at an exhibition. But the decision did not please everyone, for many were worried that a player could have his earnings adversely affected by a decision made largely by his fellow players, who could clearly benefit by their action. It was a situation unlikely to be sanctioned by the law of the land.

After this World Championship the WSPBA decided to alter the world ranking system, with effect from the 1983 championships. They planned to base it on the results of selected open tournaments, rather than on the World Championship results alone. One of the ranking tournaments was the Jameson International, in which, in 1982, Tony Knowles registered his first major tournament victory. He had a 9-6 victory in the final over David Taylor, who had beaten Steve Davis in an earlier round.

Davis withdrew from the next competition, the new Professional Players Tournament (which has since become the Rothmans Grand Prix), which also carried ranking points. This tournament was originally inaugurated by the WPBSA to enable the players to earn some of the money which was now coming in from sponsorship and television deals. (The WPBSA had decided to control all snooker's television contracts after Davis and Griffiths had played an 'unofficial' challenge match on ITV; they had also screened a Tolly Cobbold Classic in opposition to a BBC snooker match.) Therefore, the Professional Players Tournament was deliberately not sponsored or televised. The WPBSA was trying to unload its wealth, not get richer.

Ray Reardon won the first tournament, beating Jimmy White 10-5 in the final, so registering his first major win since 1978. Despite the public's lack of enthusiasm at the International Snooker Club in Aston, there were only two of these tournaments before a sponsor and television did in fact become associated with the tournament. So even when the snooker authorities were trying to get rid of their surplus money to the players, they succeeded only in making more. The game was truly a golden goose.

In the 1982 Coral UK Championship, Terry Griffiths, having beaten Steve Davis in the quarter-final, took the title with a brilliant 16-15 victory over Alex Higgins, winning the last three frames from 15-13 down. Then came the new World Doubles Championship. Sponsored by Hofmeister, the first championship was held at Crystal Palace, where the vast open spaces were quite wrong for snooker. It was won by the Hearn stablemates Steve Davis and Tony Meo, who had a crushing 13-2 final victory over the Welsh pair Terry Griffiths and Doug Mountjoy. ITV screened the event, which was to prove popular.

Cliff Thorburn, one of the heroes of the Crucible, who always seems to be involved in great matches, and whose 147 came in a match which ended with dawn breaking.

Steve Davis, who had won the Langs Scottish Classic early in the season, but was not World or even UK Champion, now won the Lada Classic by beating the giant Bill Werbeniuk 9-5 at the Spectrum Arena, Warrington, which turned into a popular snooker venue. And Cliff Thorburn finally came back to something like his best form, with a victory in the Benson and Hedges Masters, his second favourite tournament after the Embassy World Championship. He beat Ray Reardon 9-7.

Thorburn was involved in all the great matches of the World Championship at the Crucible in 1983, but was not to be the winner. His second-round match with Terry Griffiths was among the most extraordinary ever seen. One of the great

Kirk Stevens always seemed to be on the wrong end of close results in the 1980s, even losing to Cliff Thorburn in the quarter final of the 1983 World Championship after being two up with three to play.

events of televised snooker occurred in the fourth frame. Cliff missed a red into a top pocket, which came back along the cushion to pot a red into the opposite pocket. From this fluke he compiled the only 147 break so far made in the World Championship. The excitement was so great, as he neared the magic figure, that play even stopped on the other table at the Crucible; Cliff's fellow-Canadian Bill Werbeniuk, whose match was in progress, was seen poking his head round the dividing screen to watch his mate make history. The break earned Thorburn a bonus of £10,000, plus £3,000 for the highest tournament break.

Thorburn led Griffiths for the most of the match, and was 8-6 ahead when the final session started. Unluckily for Thorburn, it could not start until 8.55 pm because the previous match, in which Eddie Charlton had beaten John Spencer 13-11, had overrun. Neither Griffiths nor Thorburn are players to give much away, and Thorburn had to wait until well past 2 am for an opportunity to win at 12-9, but he missed a black and failed to clinch the frame. It was nearly 3 am before he had a chance to win the next frame, but again he missed a black, and Griffiths had levelled at 12-12. Long before this, the BBC overtime purse was empty, and the television crews and commentators had all gone to bed. Only a few spectators remained for the final frame. Cliff's nerve held in the decider, and he made a 75 break to win 13-12. The time – 3.51 am. The match had lasted 13 hours 15 minutes and prompted the WPBSA to introduce a rule allowing play to be suspended at 1 am and resumed the following day.

If this was not enough, Thorburn had another tremendous struggle with Kirk Stevens in the quarter-final. At 12-10 he was two down with three frames to play, but won them all. This time the final frame took over an hour and the match finished at 2.12 am. Once again, Thorburn had had to play a session of over six hours to win a match.

Thorburn was back in action the next day, playing Tony Knowles over 31 frames in the semi-final. Incredibly, Thorburn was again two down with three to play, and again won the last three frames to win 16-15. These matches must have contributed not a little to those interesting bags under Cliff's eyes.

It was not surprising that Thorburn could not produce his best against Steve Davis in the final. Davis had been rarely extended in his half of the draw, and his semi-final with Higgins ended a session early. Thorburn lost 18-6, but through will-power as well as his talent had put himself back on the top level.

Steve Davis consolidated his No. 1 ranking when the 1983–84 season began by winning the first two tournaments, the Langs Scottish Masters and the Jameson International, both without being seriously extended. But he crashed in the Professional Players Tournament when Mike Hallett, producing one of those performances which he frequently promises but only occasionally delivers, beat him 5-2 in the second round. As so often happens when the underdog beats the favourite, he is unable to sustain his form, and in this case Hallett lost 5-3 to Tony Meo in the next round.

The event was notable for the best performance, after four years as a professional, of the Bradford player, Joe Johnson. He beat White, Charlton, Thorburn and Meo to reach the final against Tony Knowles, and after being

1-6 down, fought back to force a deciding frame at 8-8. Unluckily for Johnson, Knowles then stopped a run of four losing frames to win the last and the championship 9-8.

Steve Davis' defeat by Hallett appeared to be no more than a hiccup as the Coral UK Championship progressed. He stormed to the final by winning 36 of the 48 frames necessary to get him there. His opponent was Alex Higgins in what promised to be an exciting match. Higgins, since his emotional World Championship victory 18 months earlier, when he had hugged his wife and baby, and cried with joy, had fought with his wife and gone through the trauma of divorce proceedings and the prospect of losing custody of his two children. He had been so depressed that, in the previous two tournaments, he had been beaten 5-2 by two players whom he would normally expect to beat, Dave Martin and Mike Watterson. However, chances of a marriage reconciliation inspired him to recover from 0-4 in his first-round match with Murdo McLeod to win 9-6, and with his wife back home he then proceeded to the final as easily as Davis.

It had been seven matches and nearly four years since Higgins had last beaten Davis, and when the World Champion began with six breaks between 54 and 84 in the first session to lead by 7-0, it looked as if the Irishman would be buried again. But Higgins, in the evening session, was brilliant, and played with a calculated determination that he rarely achieves. Risky flamboyant shots were for once ignored as he clawed his way back into the match with superb safety play. He ended that evening session only 8-7 down, and might actually have taken all eight frames had not Davis fluked a yellow in the frame he won.

Joe Johnson's first notable performance was to get to the final of the Professional Players Tournament in 1983, where he fought back from 1-6 to level with Tony Knowles, but lost.

Higgins won the first frame on the last day, which was the second birthday of the daughter he had held as World Champion at the Crucible, and as the last evening session began the scores were 11-11. This was a very significant match in the career of Steve Davis. Frequently before he had beaten players by 9-0 or 5-0; even players of the calibre of Terry Griffiths, Dennis Taylor, and Jimmy White had lost 9-0 to him. In those matches he had betrayed no emotion as he annihilated his opponents – it appeared that he took each frame separately, whatever the score. Davis seemed to have the perfect temperament. But, as Higgins fought back in this match, it was obvious that Davis was very much affected by the score, almost as if a deep sense of fatalism had descended upon him.

Higgins went ahead at 14-12, but then lost his touch, allowing Davis, who was still not playing well, to win three frames and lead 15-14, with one more needed for the championship. Higgins, now on the brink of defeat, regained his spirit, and from then on victory seemed almost inevitable, particularly when Davis missed a black which could have wrapped it up. Higgins levelled at 15-15, and seized his chance in the final frame when Davis missed a red. Higgins, revelling in the 'pressure', controlled the frame from then on to lead 70-0, and won an exciting match. For Davis, the match must have raised questions he had not considered since he had begun his career, and the echoes of this match were no doubt still reverberating in his brain when another Irishman, Dennis Taylor, was repeating the 'recovery horror' at the Crucible some 16 months later.

Davis won the Hofmeister World Doubles in 1983 with his friend Tony Meo, when Knowles and White were beaten 10-2 in the final. This tournament was notable for an incident in the semi-final in which Knowles and White were playing Virgo and Thorburn. Knowles fouled, and Virgo, after looking at the table, asked him to play again. Knowles did so, at which Thorburn potted a red only to be penalised by the referee for playing out of turn.

Davis and Meo were the finalists in the Lada Classic, which was now an open tournament and consequently carried ranking points. The young John Parrott from Liverpool, in his first professional season, made a big impression in this tournament, beating Mountjoy, Higgins and Knowles before losing a little unluckily 5-4 to Davis in the semi-final. The near-triumph of the 19-year-old overshadowed a similar one of a 47-year-old Mark Wildman, who also reached his first semi-final.

The Davis-Meo final was marred by a spectator. Meo, who had not beaten Davis in a tournament, seemed about to do so when he needed to clear the colours to the pink in the final frame. It was not difficult, but a cry of 'Come on Tony' from a spectator as he was about to play the yellow clearly put him off, enabling Davis to take the title 9-8.

Tony Meo appeared to add to his stature as a player when he partnered Steve Davis in the Hofmeister World Doubles Championship. He was often the dominant player as they won four of the first five tournaments.

Opposite: Steve Davis and Alex Higgins before the second day of the Coral UK Championship final in 1983. This was the match in which Davis lost a 7-0 lead and opened up new hope for all his opponents, which Dennis Taylor, in particular, was to profit from.

The greatest moment in Kirk Stevens' career came in the Benson & Hedges Masters semi-final in 1984. Stevens made a televised 147, but in one of the best matches of recent years, he lost again.

The most talked-about match of the season was played in the Benson and Hedges Masters. Jimmy White met Kirk Stevens in a semi-final filled with outstanding snooker, as both players potted at the top of their form. White made a break of 113 to move into a 5-3 lead, needing one more frame for victory. The next frame, however, proved to be Kirk Stevens' finest hour, as he made a televised 147. His joy was unbounded, and lasted throughout the next frame, even though White came back to win the match with a break of 119. But even defeat could not dampen Kirk's euphoria, and the two players left the arena the most delighted of opponents. White maintained his form to take the Masters title with a 9-5 victory over Griffiths.

Steve Davis retained the Benson and Hedges Irish Masters and Tolly Cobbold Classic in devastating style, and was a firmer favourite than ever when the 1984 World Championship came round. White and Stevens had another great match in the semi-final, with White coming from behind this time. He was 12-10 down as the final session started, but came through by 16-14.

This great match seemed to have taken the stuffing out of White when the final against Steve Davis started. In the 16 frames played on the first day he could win only four. He was just over 22 years old, and it was his last opportunity to win the world title at a younger age than Alex Higgins, who had clinched it 12 years before. Higgins was very much his idol, and Alex admired the young Londoner in return, even lending him a suit for the final. An overnight score of 12-4 to Davis, with neither player performing particularly well, did not suggest a great finish.

White began the next day, however, as if he realized that his situation could hardly get worse, and he played in his usual uninhibited style. A break of 119 in the first frame set the standard, and the crowd began to get excited as frame by frame was pulled back. Jimmy won seven of the eight frames in the afternoon session (just as Higgins had done against Davis in the Coral UK), and left the arena only 13-11 down.

Steve Davis, who has made a habit of starting impressively after a break, moved ahead 16-12, but White again cut into the lead and at last got to within one frame of him at 17-16. There were two frames left, and had he got level he must have been favourite in the decider. But Davis, with his one-frame cushion, was just the stronger in the next frame, and took the championship 18-16. He was the first player to retain the title at the Crucible, and had now been World Champion three times in four years.

The 1983–84 season had seen an attempt at a Professional Snooker League. It involved 12 players and 66 matches, each one consisting of ten frames, with two points for a win and one for a draw. The players invited by Professional Snooker League Ltd. were the top 12 in the rankings, but Barry Hearn, on behalf of Steve Davis and Terry Griffiths, declined to participate on the grounds that the money was not good enough. Cliff Thorburn also declined, as he was living in Canada, and Meo, of the Barry Hearn stable, turned down an invitation as a replacement. As it happened, two of the substitutes, John Virgo and Dennis Taylor, finished first and second respectively. The League was not repeated in the following season.

Steve Davis began the 1984–85 season in his usual brilliant style. He took the Langs Supreme Scottish Masters for the third year in succession, beating White 9-5 in the final, and then won the Jameson International very impressively, crushing Knowles 9-2 in the final. Davis won 33 frames in this competition, while losing only eight. (It was his third victory in four years in this competition.)

Dennis Taylor had looked impressive in the Jameson, but was forced to scratch in the quarter-final because his mother died suddenly. He returned to the circuit for the Rothmans Grand Prix, which took over from the Professional Players Tournament, and, playing with a more serious demeanour than usual and, it seemed, great determination, again looked impressive. He was now wearing new 'inverted' spectacles, which allowed him to look through the lenses at the correct angle when he bent over the cue. He advanced very comfortably to the

Steve Davis and Jimmy White before the 1984 World Championship final. White had his last chance to become the youngest ever Champion, but despite a tremendous fightback he lost 18-16.

final, where he met Cliff Thorburn, who had stopped Davis' run with a 9-7 semi-final defeat.

After the first four frames of the final had been shared, Dennis took the next eight for a 10-2 win. It was a very emotional victory for a popular player who asked his young son to join him in the spotlight for the victory celebrations. Taylor had been a professional since 1971 and, although he had won the Irish Professional Championship in 1982, this was his first major victory. As he pointed out, he could now see! Over the years he had played with and without spectacles, and had tried contact lenses. His new outsize glasses did the trick.

The Coral UK Championship became the Coral Open in 1984–85, to allow players who did not hold British passports to enter. Because the Coral sponsorship contract had run since 1978, with the same prize money, Hearn was considering pulling out Steve Davis, since he did not think the sum was now high enough. However, lack of money was compensated for by the ranking points, which ensured a top quality field to keep the BBC audiences happy.

Davis and Higgins reached the final, as they had the year before, but not without incident. Higgins' victory over Thorburn in the semi-final demonstrated an inflexibility in the rules, or at least in referee

The fastest cues in the west, Jimmy White and Alex Higgins, teamed up in 1984 to break the monopoly that Davis and Meo have otherwise established on the Hofmeister World Doubles Championship.

John Smyth. Thorburn led 6-5 and, in the next frame, snookered himself behind the pack of reds. He nominated the green ball and played himself neatly out of the predicament. Referee Smyth did not hear the nomination and, thinking that Thorburn had not nominated a colour at all, penalized him seven points. Some of the audience protested, as did Thorburn, who appealed to Higgins to support him, but Higgins said he had not heard the call. Yet the nomination of the green was picked up clearly by the television microphones. The referee did not accept the evidence of the spectators, as he is entitled to do by the rules, while Thorburn angrily told Higgins that he could not borrow his cue extension, which Higgins had been using throughout the match. Nonetheless, Higgins went on to win the frame, the next two, and eventually the match by 9-7.

The 1984 final began like the previous year's, with Davis playing brilliantly to lead 8-2. Then Higgins, as before, began a comeback which won him six frames to Davis' one, and took him to only 9-8 down. This time, however, he could not get the frame which would put him level, nor did he have the inspiration of the previous year, and Steve steadily pulled away. In fact, Alex did not win another frame as Steve took seven consecutively to win the title 16-8.

This was a period when there was a new look to more than one event in the calendar, and the Hofmeister World Doubles produced new champions after Davis and Meo had looked almost unbeatable since the event was inaugurated. This year they were beaten in the semi-final 9-6 by Higgins and White. The 'Hurricane' and the 'Whirlwind' then went on to blow away Thorburn and Thorne in the final 10-2. The two players whose images most recall the smoky billiards halls of the old-time hustlers looked odd as they appeared in identical ritzy suits, Beverley Sisters style.

The new look in the Spectrum Arena, Warrington, came from the Mercantile Credit Company taking over the sponsorship of the Lada Classic. The two losers in the Hofmeister Doubles fought out the final. Willie Thorne had built a reputation as a brilliant player on the practice tables, but one who lacked the nerve to win the big matches. In the semi-final he had his best win since turning professional ten years earlier when he beat Steve Davis 9-8. Cliff Thorburn had a much easier semi-final, beating Joe Johnson 9-2. Johnson, in his first televised semi-final, confirmed his reputation for not being able to play in front of the cameras, a reputation which he sensationally exploded 15 months later.

Willie Thorne, breakbuilder extraordinary, finally broke through by beating Cliff Thorburn in the 1985 Mercantile Credit Classic. He played some brilliant snooker to win.

The Thorne *v* Thorburn final produced some of the best snooker ever seen simultaneously from both players. In the 15 frames of the first day there were 13 breaks of over 40, including three centuries. Thorne led 8-7, but Thorburn levelled with the first frame of the following day. From then on the match took a new turn, however, as Thorburn began to miss the occasional pot, and Thorne, bubbling over with confidence, found a new ability in safety play to add to his breakbuilding skills. He took five frames running, to end as a 13-8 winner. It was Thorne's first major victory.

Cliff Thorburn had quick compensation by retaining the Benson and Hedges Masters, beating Doug Mountjoy 9-6 in the final. Higgins found himself in trouble again with the WPBSA when over-exultant remarks, after he had beaten Davis in the first round, contained an expletive which was picked up by the television microphones. He was fined £1,500 for this outburst. But possibly more disagreeable was the rowdyism among his supporters who had booed Davis' entrance. Higgins and White appeared to have acquired the sort of fans which snooker could do without, and which suggested that Wembley might not be an ideal venue for the game.

Another new tournament with another new winner, and, unfortunately, another new scandal, followed with the Dulux British Open. It was held at the Derby Assembly Rooms, where the Yamaha Organs event had previously been held. The new tournament carried a then record £50,000 prize for the winner, ranking points, and ITV coverage. Independent television has not covered snooker (or indeed any other sport) as well as BBC, and in this event insisted that the televised phase from the second round to quarter-finals be the best of nine frames. Since the qualifying and first round were the best of 11 frames this was utterly illogical, and should not have been agreed to by the WPBSA. The requirements of television and sponsors alone should not be allowed to influence the conditions or rules of a tournament. The absurd result was that Steve Davis, the World Champion, could win the last two frames to beat Tony Chappel 6-5 in the first round, whereas had the match been in the second round, Chappel would have registered the biggest surprise of the year with a 5-4 victory.

Lesser surprises in the semi-finals involved Kirk Stevens, who beat Steve Davis 9-7, and Silvino Francisco, who beat Alex Higgins 9-6, ensuring that the eventual winner would be scoring a first-ever major tournament success. In addition this was the first time that a major tournament final had not been contested by a player from the British Isles.

Silvino Francisco, of South Africa, beat the Canadian 12-9, but it was events off the table which kept the snooker world talking for the next 12 months. Francisco thought that Stevens was using drugs and protested during the match to the tournament director. When no action was taken, an angry Francisco followed Stevens to the toilets on the second day where there was an altercation. None of this came to public notice at the time, but remarks by Francisco had been noted (and tape-recorded) by a tabloid newspaper, and they were published on the morning of his first match in the 1985 World Championship.

Before that, however, the World Cup, whose television spot was taken over by the Rothmans Grand Prix in 1984, was revived with sponsorship from Guinness. It was played at the Bournemouth Conference Centre, where there were new winners. Previously, Wales, England and Canada had won the three-man team event, but now Ireland registered their first win. Alex Higgins, Dennis Taylor and Eugene Hughes made up the winning trio. Jimmy White, however, won the Benson and Hedges Irish Masters, with a 9-5 final victory over Alex Higgins.

With the snooker circus gathered at the Crucible for that year's World Championship, the story of Francisco's allegations was published. Pressure was put on Francisco to call a press conference at which he denied the story. Not surprisingly, with so much pressure on him, he lost his first-round match with Dennis Taylor 10-2. The WPBSA then charged Francisco with physical and mental abuse of Stevens, with giving an unauthorised interview, and with delaying the final of the Dulux tournament. These charges were made only after the newspaper revelations. In May, over two months after the event, Francisco was fined £6,000 and had two ranking points deducted.

This severe punishment from a body many of whose members could gain from this ruling received much criticism. It was made to look even harsher when, in June, it was revealed that Stevens had had drug problems and was able to continue playing only after treatment in a Canadian clinic. Francisco, meanwhile, had taken legal advice and the WPBSA was shamed into cancelling its decision and putting the case before an independent tribunal.

The case was heard by Gavin Lightman QC, whose judgement in March 1986 was that Francisco should be fined £2,000 with £1,500 costs. No ranking points were to be deducted. But though the fine was reduced, the South African lost out in other ways, and had a poor year for a player of his status. The WPBSA also came out of it badly, for its ability to deal with disciplinary matters of this sort looked questionable.

There were few shocks as the World Championship progressed. Interest was created by the progress of John Parrott through to the quarter-final, where he met Ray Reardon in a classic 'experience *v* promise' encounter. The 20-year-old Parrott led 4-0 and remained ahead until, from 9-5 down, the 52-year-old Reardon, playing some of his best snooker for a long time, took seven frames on the run to lead 12-9, with one more frame needed. Parrott then rallied to 12-12, but in the deciding frame impetuous youth left a free ball on the final red and experience won the day.

Two men won through to the final without a scare – Steve Davis and Dennis Taylor. Both won their semi-finals a session early by 16-5, Davis over Reardon, and Taylor over Knowles. So, for the first time for three years, neither player could claim that his opponent was the fresher when the final started.

Silvino Francisco with his Dulux British Open trophy, 1985, the beaten finalist, Kirk Stevens, and the sponsor's publicity dog. The smiles hid the heartache of a drugs allegation.

The finalists in the Goya Matchroom Trophy of 1985, Cliff Thorburn and Jimmy White, flanking referee Len Ganley. Thorburn's recovery was one of the greatest in recent matches.

The match developed into the most exciting anybody has ever seen, although it promised to be anything but that as the first session got under way. Steve played with his usual cool mastery to run up an 8-0 lead. Dennis tried to look impassive, too, but as frame after frame slipped away a stony dejection settled on his face. Dennis has always been a popular player, but since his first-ever win earlier in the year in the Rothmans Grand Prix he had become a particular favourite with the television public. He was, however, regarded more as a nice guy than a winner, and many felt sorry for him as he appeared about to be humiliated. This made his subsequent fight back more exciting.

Taylor just won the ninth frame, but lost the next to make the score 9-1. Another long frame went to Taylor, and then he began to play in earnest. A 98 clearance was the highlight as he took the last six frames of the first day to finish, overnight, at just 9-7 down.

The public who had bought tickets for the second day and had been wondering how much they would see, were delighted when Taylor now fought his way back to 11-11. Taylor, however, could not quite get in front. Davis won two frames on the black, and the final pulsating session began with the champion 13-11 ahead. Taylor again got level at 15-15, but then Davis once more took two frames to lead 17-15. He now needed but one more frame to win. Dennis, however, took the next two to a great roar, and the championship went right to the last frame.

Taylor edged ahead, but then Davis took the lead and, with four colours left, Taylor needed them all for victory. He brilliantly potted the brown, blue and pink, but a double on the black just missed. Davis played a cool safety shot, then Taylor tried another risky double but missed again. Davis played another safety shot, but not so well, and Taylor had a long pot into a baulk pocket for the title. He missed, and this time left Davis the easiest opportunity so far, a cut-back into the top pocket. It was, however, not quite as easy as Taylor, who had walked back to his chair looking devastated, thought. Davis overcut it, touched his forehead in anguish, and Taylor potted the black for victory.

Davis looked pale and shell-shocked, while Taylor could not disguise his delight. This match was just what the WPBSA needed after the revelations of the previous few days. It marked a new high in television audiences: 18½ million had stayed up for the highest-ever post-midnight television audience in Britain, and it was the highest audience ever for BBC2.

Soon after collecting the £60,000 cheque, Taylor joined Davis under the managership of Barry Hearn, and looked forward to making his first million. With the British 'close' season now being an opportunity for the leading players to spread the game overseas and make more money, Taylor found himself travelling to the Far East and breaking new ground in China. In 1985 other leading British players also toured, heading for South America, Australia, Africa and Europe.

When the 1985–86 season started, multi-millionaire Davis found that he had too many commitments to play in the Langs Scottish Masters, which he had won in the previous three seasons. Cliff Thorburn took the opportunity to make the sort of start Davis usually made to the season, beating Thorne 9-7 in the final, and playing as well as he ever had.

In the same season the Jameson became the Goya Matchroom Trophy. Goya International linked up with Barry Hearn's stable of players and launched the Matchroom range of men's toiletries, named after Barry Hearn's club. The venue was switched to the Trentham Gardens in Stoke, and ranking points were at stake.

Alas, for Hearn, the Matchroom professionals were all eliminated before the final, which was a remarkable match between Cliff Thorburn and Jimmy White. Thorburn claimed that the first session produced the finest snooker there had ever been. He was not boasting – it all came from White, who led 7-0. But in an extraordinary eighth frame Thorburn began to turn the tide. White led 74-0 with four reds remaining, when Thorburn was awarded a free ball. He forced two more fouls and another free ball, and finally cleared the table with a break of 42 to win on the black. This is believed to be the biggest turn-round in one frame in professional snooker, and the effect on White was to undermine the confidence with which he had been potting every available ball. The 'grinder' edged back to only 8-6 down overnight, and next day clinched the title by 12-10. Goya changed their policy and withdrew from sponsorship after this one tournament.

The Rothmans Grand Prix produced another exciting final. Thorburn's run of victories was stopped in the semi-final when Steve Davis beat him 9-5. Dennis Taylor beat Tony Knowles 9-6 in the other semi-final, so the final was a repeat of the World Championship, this time with Taylor as defending champion.

The match began in a similar way, with Davis streaking to a 7-2 lead. With the winner requiring only ten frames to win, Taylor had to get to work, and he did so in style, reeling off six frames in a row to take an 8-7 lead. Perhaps this was his undoing. In the World Championship he had refrained from taking the lead until the final frame, when no comeback was possible. Now he missed an easy red as he looked likely to win another frame, allowing Davis to step in to level the game. Once again the match went into a final frame, at 9-9, but this time it was Davis whose nerve held. He won at 2.14 am.

Such was the life-style of the top snooker professionals that he pocketed the cheque for £50,000 (or, rather, handed it to Hearn), put in an appearance at the 3.30 am official reception and, without bothering with bed, left for Canada four hours later for yet more snooker. He met Dennis Taylor in another final, it being Dennis' turn to win this time.

Davis returned to appear in another final in the Coral UK, but with a new

Steve Davis in play against Willie Thorne in the final of the Coral UK Championship of 1985. If ever a single shot turned a match, it was the famous blue that Willie missed into a centre pocket.

opponent. Willie Thorne had a marvellous run through to the final, beating John Virgo 9-8 in a splendid match of five centuries, three to the loser, and then registering 9-7 wins over Thorburn, Griffiths and Dennis Taylor.

Thorne, playing with great confidence in the final, took an 8-6 lead on the first day, and the only surprise was that Davis kept in touch. Thorne had tremendous support at Preston, including the speculative financial variety. A man who likes a flutter himself, he had attracted a following of keen gamblers who had been profiting on his form all week, and looked to make another dent in the sponsor's profits in the final.

On the second day Willie felt good and played even better. He won the first two frames from 50 behind, then made 115 and 61 clearances to go 12-6 up. But at 13-8, just three frames from victory, Willie ran into trouble. Clearing up again after a Davis break of 46, he strolled around the table, nonchalantly potting the colours as he had been all day. An easy blue from its spot into the middle pocket would have made it 14-8. Willie went to pot it, intending to follow up with the pink from its spot – it was all too easy. He could hardly believe it when the blue rattled the jaw and failed to drop. All that dropped was Willie's jaw. Davis, too, sat in his seat in disbelief for a while, before stepping forward to claim the frame.

Thorne's touch then deserted him as Davis took five in a row to level and then wrapped it up at 16-14. Thorne was shaken, and so were his backers, who were less than generous with their applause for Steve Davis' fightback.

Ray Reardon, who so far had won only two matches in the 1985–86 British season (he had tried Taylor-like spectacles the year before) had a good run in the Hofmeister World Doubles, partnering Tony Jones of England, who played extremely well under the eye of the old master. The holders, Higgins and White, went out early, and Davis and Meo had no difficulty in getting 'their' title back with a 12-5 final win over Reardon and Jones, who at last ran out of steam.

The makers of Kit Kat, the chocolate bar, presumably thinking that their slogan 'Have a break, have a Kit Kat' suggested snooker, sponsored a new event in 1985 – the Kit Kat Break for World Champions. It was open to the eight World Champions still playing competitive snooker: Fred Davis, Ray Reardon, John Spencer, Alex Higgins, Terry Griffiths, Cliff Thorburn, Steve Davis and Dennis Taylor. At the East Midlands Conference Centre, Nottingham, the £10,000 first prize went to Dennis Taylor, the reigning champion.

The Mercantile Credit Classic produced another classic final between Jimmy White and Cliff Thorburn, echoing the Goya earlier in the season. Jimmy went away again to a 4-0 lead, but Cliff got to 4-3 when Jimmy had to concede a frame for being two minutes late for the evening session. Before he had recovered his poise he was 6-4 behind. The second day began with Thorburn leading 8-7.

White started brilliantly again and went 11-9 ahead, but Thorburn does not give in and levelled at 12-12. Yet another final went to the last frame, but this one was to have a closer finish than any yet. With Cliff well ahead in the decider, he rashly attempted a black along the top cushion which would have almost guaranteed victory. It stayed out, and gave Jimmy a chance, but it was a slight one. With four balls left on the table he needed a snooker, and when he potted brown and blue it looked like a miscalculation. But with just pink and black left Jimmy laid a perfect snooker, with the pink in the middle of the table and the cue ball tucked behind the black. Cliff missed, and Jimmy proceeded to pot both pink and black for his first-ever ranking tournament victory.

Thorburn did not have to wait long for revenge. The Benson and Hedges Masters saw him and Jimmy White meet in their third final of the season. White had beaten Steve Davis in the semi-final for his third victory over him in four meetings. Thorburn won 9-5 to retain his Masters title, also becoming the first to win it three times.

Steve Davis tuned up nicely for the World Championship with a fairly comfortable victory in the Dulux British Open, in which he beat Willie Thorne 12-7 in the final. Ireland retained their World Cup, now sponsored by Car Care Plan, by beating Canada 9-7 in the final, and Jimmy White won the Benson and Hedges Irish Masters, Willie Thorne being the 9-5 losing finalist.

At the Crucible, Davis, determined to regain his world title, came fairly comfortably through his half of the draw until meeting Thorburn in the semi-final. The match was a brilliant scrap between the two best players in the world, but from 12-12 the close frames all went to

Jimmy White with the Mercantile Credit Classic trophy in 1986. It was White's first victory in a ranking tournament, won on the last black in another of his brilliant matches with Cliff Thorburn.

Steve, who entered the final by 16-12.

The other half of the draw was wide open from the first round, when Dennis Taylor suffered the reaction not unknown to previous champions, and was eliminated by Mike Hallett. Hallett led 8-1 at the interval and held off Taylor's recovery to win 10-6. Terry Griffiths looked the likeliest player to reach the final, but he slipped up against the No.16 seed, Joe Johnson, who had beaten Hallett. Griffiths had beaten Higgins 13-12, and led 12-9 against Johnson. But Johnson made two century breaks in taking the last four frames to win 13-12. When Johnson beat Knowles 16-8 in the semi-finals, the final looked to be a formality. Johnson had been 150-1 against in the betting at the start – even when he reached the final, backers could have had 5-1.

Centuries in successive frames took

Joe Johnson shook up the snooker establishment in 1986 by winning the World Championship, and proving that at the top level there was not much between the players.

Davis to 3-1, three in a row put Johnson ahead at 4-3, four in a row for Davis made it 7-4, then four in a row for Johnson made it 8-7. They finished the first day at 8-8, and Johnson must have been delighted with his form.

Wearing jazzy two-tone shoes Johnson led 12-8 at the first interval next day, and held on to take a 13-11 lead into the last session. Even so, few expected him to win. He was playing in an unhurried manner, going for his shots, and the feeling was that the enormity of what he was on the brink of achieving must hit him shortly. Yet he won the first frame of the final evening session, and gave every sign that he was enjoying playing in the final, which was a big achievement for him, and that winning it would be no more than an unexpected bonus. He had not a care in the world. The last evidence of resistance from the understandably rattled Davis faded when he failed to clear the colours to prevent Johnson going 16-12 ahead. Soon Johnson was making a break of 64 which virtually guaranteed him the title, and the smile on his face as he potted the last few colours, knowing that he could afford to miss, showed how much he was enjoying it. He was generous in victory and a very popular winner. But Davis could take consolation from the fact that the public enjoyed his defeats so much only because he was such an excellent player. Another consolation might have been, of course, his £244,333 winnings for the season, a record.

The 1986–87 season began with Thorburn retaining his Langs Scottish Masters title with a fighting comeback against Alex Higgins in the final. He took the last two frames to win 9-8. The new World Champion, Joe Johnson, lost 5-2 to Higgins in the quarter-final. Jimmy White took part, having become the latest member of the Barry Hearn Matchroom group. The other six Matchroom players – Davis, Meo, Griffiths, Taylor, Thorne, and Neal Foulds – took part instead in a new Matchroom Trophy created specially for them alone at the Cliffs Pavilion, Southend. A number of sponsors had been gathered together by Hearn, and £100,000 was available in prize money, compared to £40,000 for the Langs.

Tony Knowles, whose World Championship semi-final defeat in 1986 was his third at this stage of the tournament. Knowles has not been able to translate his talents into victories.

Willie Thorne came from behind to win the last three frames of the final to beat Steve Davis 10-9 and win his biggest cheque so far of £50,000. Rex Williams, the WPBSA chairman, was quoted as saying that he would be worried if too many top class players came under one management.

BCE (Billiard Cues of England), makers of the tables used in tournaments, took over the sponsorship of what had been the Goya International. A new tournament rule that no frame may be started within 40 minutes of the time the next session was scheduled to begin had possible crucial effects on two matches: in the fifth round Terry Griffiths came from 4-1 down against Cliff Thorburn to level at 4-4, but the final frame was postponed until after the next session. Griffiths' winning streak was interrupted, and he lost 5-4.

In the quarter-final between Eugene Hughes and Steve Davis, Hughes led 4-2, but Davis made rapid breaks of 74 and 59 to win the next two frames. Davis desperately tried to win these frames within the time limit so that he could finish off the match while in the ascendancy, but Hughes successfully prolonged the frames to force the last one to be postponed. He then won it for his most important victory to date.

Hughes led 7-6 in his semi-final with Neal Foulds, but lost 9-8. Foulds' final opponent was the ever-present Cliff Thorburn. Thorburn led, but on the second day began to have trouble with his tip, being forced to take a 15-minute time-out to change it. He could not find his touch, and at 12-9, Foulds, who had played exceptionally well all week, won his first major title.

The Rothmans Grand Prix was notable for the performances of a veteran and a newcomer. The newcomer, 17-year-old Stephen Hendry, all but beat Jimmy White in the quarter-final, missing a blue in the final frame when needing the last three colours. The veteran was Rex Williams, who reached the final against Jimmy White. Williams led 6-4 before White reeled off the last six frames for a 10-6 win.

The UK Open also obtained a new sponsor in the 1986–87 season. Tennents took over the ranking tournament at Preston. Hendry again announced his class with a brilliant match with Higgins, which went to the final frame. Hendry made a break of 54 but missed a red, and Higgins, in a style which has become familiar, cleared to the pink with a break of 82 to win by 9-8. Another young player, John Parrott, beat world champion Joe Johnson 9-1.

One of the discoveries of the 1986–87 season was Stephen Hendry, a 17-year-old who appeared to have all the necessary qualities to go to the top.

There was nearly a sensation in the quarter-final when Tony Drago, potting like a genius, forced a deciding frame with Steve Davis at 8-8, and led 54-1. Davis then made a break of 40, but broke down with only the colours on the table, leaving Drago needing only the baulk colours and with a fairly easy yellow to start. Alas, the shot needed the rest, and an over-excited Drago – not taking time to compose himself – missed badly and Davis won.

Neal Foulds, who turned out to be his final opponent, had enjoyed superior form all season, but Davis won the final fairly comfortably 16-7. He was certainly the form man for the tournament, for this was his fifth win, the third in succession.

Stephen Hendry proved himself the find of the season by reaching a final. Mike Hallett was his partner in the Hofmeister World Doubles, and the pair, 100-1 at the start of the event, put out three seeded pairs to meet Davis and Meo in the final. They played well, but only just managed to extend the final into a second day. Davis and Meo won 12-3, taking the title for the fourth time in its five-year history.

Cliff Thorburn failed to win the Masters title for a third successive year when he was beaten, in an exciting semi-final, by Dennis Taylor 5-4. Thorburn was ahead in the deciding frame when Taylor made a mistake on the yellow, but flukily snookered Thorburn. Thorburn left the yellow on, and Taylor took all the colours to win. Taylor then made another exciting late-night recovery in the final against Alex Higgins. Needing the last four frames to win, he looked like losing 9-5 when Higgins led 40-0 in the 14th frame, but Alex made a mess of a risky safety shot, and Dennis stepped in to begin his fightback. It ended at 1.09 am in a victory at 9-8, and his first Masters title.

The Dulux Open final was fought out by the two most successful players of the season to date, Jimmy White and Neal Foulds, White winning 13-9. Unofficial rankings indicated that these two were in line to move up to second and fourth in the ranking list, with just the World Championship itself to come.

The pre-World Championship story concerned the banishment of Alex Higgins. The decision was announced of the one-man tribunal appointed by the WPBSA to look into charges that he had head-butted Paul Hatherell, the WPBSA executive who was tournament director of the Tennents UK Championship. Higgins was to be fined £12,000 and banned from five tournaments.

A more far-reaching story concerned the use of drugs, and specifically those known as beta-blockers, which slow down the heartbeat, thus not only calming the nerves of players but giving them a better chance of striking the ball without even the distraction of a heart-beat putting them off the stroke. Rex Williams, the Chairman of the WPBSA, and Neal Foulds, at the time the most successful player of the season, admitted taking the drugs, having been prescribed them. The WPBSA's position was that the drugs were allowable if prescribed for a medical condition. This attitude is not accepted in most sports, as it is known that medical certificates can be obtained for almost anything.

The Crucible itself, in accordance with the moves to tone down the connection with the sponsor's brand of cigarettes, was not in the usual Embassy red decor, but a muted blue, with the Embassy name far less prominent.

The seedings and draw meant that many of the strong players were in the bottom half of the draw, but there were soon shocks in both halves, six of the seeded players going out in the first round: Rex Williams, Kirk Stevens, Willie Thorne, Tony Knowles, Cliff Thorburn and Tony Meo. Three of their conquerors reached the quarter-finals and announced an upswing in their fortunes: Stephen Hendry, who lost his quarter-final 13-12 to World Champion Joe Johnson, and Mike Hallett and Dene O'Kane, who each beat two seeds.

Against all expectations, the final was a repeat of 1986: Johnson v Davis. Despite being in the easier half of the draw, Johnson began the tournament as a 66-1 outsider. This time Johnson led at 4-3, but Davis then pulled away to 8-4, and although Johnson twice got to within a frame he could never level, and Davis won his fourth Championship by 18-14.

Above: Steve Davis with the Embassy World Championship trophy in 1987, when he gained revenge over Joe Johnson for his 1986 defeat and took the title for the fourth time in six years. Inset: *'Look – no hands'. Davis shows his skill and control is not confined to the snooker table.*

THE BASE OF THE PYRAMID

Cliff Wilson at Pontins in 1981. Wilson is almost a reluctant professional. A hero among the clubs and institutes at Tredegar, he still gives the impression of being an amateur enjoying a serious professional game.

The snooker champion of the world is the top of a pyramid, at the bottom of which are the casual club players. The base of this pyramid is widening as snooker spreads around the world: players in China, Brazil, Hong Kong and some European countries now knock the coloured balls around the green baize.

One effect of the television boom in snooker, which has allowed multi-millionaire Steve Davis to become the richest sportsman in Great Britain, and has made a number of players into 'stars', is the new public image of the game and its players. Until the 1970s the conception of a snooker player (or billiards – or pool in America) was of somebody who had 'misspent his youth'. This was largely the influence of films. Billiards halls were portrayed as smoky, easy-going haunts which provided ideal meeting places for criminals. Paul Newman's very successful film *The Hustler* (1961) was typical of this genre, and even now American television detective drama series use the pool hall 'dive' as a typical underworld backdrop.

This conception was false, or at least grossly exaggerated, in Great Britain. Many snooker halls in the old days were in fact above a popular chain of tailor's shops. British Legion clubs usually had a snooker table, as did Conservative Clubs. And players such as Ray Reardon and Cliff Wilson learned the game in the local institutes in their home towns.

Jimmy White and Tony Meo developed their precocious skills in halls around Tooting, South London. They were so good that they toured the country in the taxi of cabbie Bob Davis, playing money matches, and winning stakes from players usually considerably older (Jimmy was then hardly in his teens), but not in the same class as themselves. 'Taxi Bob' was the stake-raiser and manager. Yet perhaps there was some truth in the old legends, for Jimmy White has been quoted as saying that villains were a part of the scenery.

While Jimmy and Tony were simultaneously learning their trade and living off their skills, even the World Championships were not the hushed, immaculate presentations they are today. Before television took over, the top matches had been played under the pool of light from the shade over the table, with spectators, if any, in the surrounding gloom. And the gloom hid the faults in the auditorium and the facilities.

The year in which the 17-year-old Jimmy White won the World Amateur Championship, 1980, was when the whole conception of snooker was finally changed. The public had seen the older players for ten years in television's *Pot Black*. But now a man they had never previously heard of, Terry Griffiths, entranced them by winning the World Championship. And two years later the young and immensely talented Steve Davis took the title. Suddenly, snooker was seen to be an exciting game for personable, articulate young men.

A qualitative change came over snooker when television hoisted it into the limelight. It was now rich, colourful and up-market. The old halls and social clubs began to give way to new snooker centres, some run by professional players. The aspiring youngster could now play in good conditions, with every opportunity, if good enough, to progress to the top. Social snooker and local leagues were still enjoyed, but now there were open competitions in which the best amateurs from a wide area could compete. Prizes were worthwhile – a good open amateur tournament could carry £1,000 or more as a first prize. The best players could meet the best competition just below the professional ranks, and for many these open tournaments were the preliminaries to a professional career. Tony Drago, the Maltese player who almost beat Steve Davis in the Tennents UK Open in 1986, used to fly to Britain for the big amateur tournaments.

In snooker, the terms 'professional' and 'amateur' do not distinguish players who are paid and those who are not, as the previous paragraph implies. A professional is a player who is a member of the WPBSA but this status is not readily given. After the Second World War the number of practising professionals did not even reach double figures. There has always been a suspicion that some players have been frowned upon, less for their competence as players than for their failure to represent the 'correct' type who can maintain the Association's image of the game. In 1986–87 there were 128 professionals eligible to compete on the circuit, a number which the Association had decided was a reasonable maximum.

Below: A modern snooker club, very functional, clean, well-lit, with a notable absence of cigarette smoke and the sort of hood associated with such halls in B movies.

Bottom: One of the top professionals who has his own club is Willie Thorne, which gives him the right to relax by sitting on one of his own tables in Leicester.

John Parrott was an excellent player at an early age and became well-known while still an amateur. Here he is playing in a local club.

While not all amateurs aspire to the professional circuit, those that do need not wait to make money from the game. Those outstanding young players who can make a name before being accepted by the WPBSA can even get endorsements or exhibition engagements and are, in effect, professionals before receiving official status. John Parrott and Steve Newbury, who turned professional in 1983 and 1984 respectively, are two players who, when 'amateur', were making more money than many professionals at the foot of the prize-money list. The best means by which an amateur can make an impact on the game still lies in winning his national championship, or, even better, the World Championship for amateurs.

The list of English Amateur Champions includes the names of four men who became World Professional Champions: John Pulman, Ray Reardon, John Spencer and Terry Griffiths. (The Welshmen Reardon and Griffiths were not barred from competing since the English Championship is open to all players.) Rex Williams, David Taylor and Jimmy White are all past winners now familiar to British television audiences, while nearly all of the winners in the last 25 years have become professionals.

Reardon and Griffiths are among the players who have won the Welsh Amateur title, together with other current top professionals Cliff Wilson and Doug Mountjoy. Scotland, however, has not produced players of this rank for a long time, and Walter Donaldson, the post-war Professional World Champion, was never Scottish Amateur Champion. Yet Stephen Hendry, the 15-year-old winner in 1984, who repeated his success in 1985, appears certain to make a big name in the professional ranks. Alex Higgins was Northern Ireland Amateur Champion, and Eugene Hughes the Republic's Amateur Champion, but Dennis Taylor, the third member of the All-Ireland World Cup-winning side in 1985, 1986 and 1987, did not win an amateur championship.

However, in other countries the National Amateur Championships have not been stepping stones to professional fame to the same extent, although some championships date as far back as just after the end of the Second World War – in the case of India and South Africa, to just before. Silvino and Peter Francisco are current leading professionals who have won South Africa's National Championships, but the most famous name in the list of Indian champions is Englishman Jimmy White. He won the title in 1980, just before turning professional. M.J.M. Lafir, of Sri Lanka, won the Indian championship eight times from 1956 to 1977, and his home championship 18 times from 1948 to 1973. Among today's better-known professionals who have won their country's amateur championship are Warren King and John Campbell (Australia), Jim Wych (Canada), Tony Drago (Malta) and Dene O'Kane (New Zealand).

Since 1963 there have been World Amateur Snooker Championships, usually every two years. The first ten winners were all English or Welsh, the most famous names among them being David Taylor, Doug Mountjoy, Cliff Wilson and Jimmy White, who was the youngest ever champion at 18 years old. There has been a change since 1984, however, with the latest winners being Omprakesh Agrawal (India) and Paul Mifsud (Malta). Agrawal became India's first professional in 1984, and in 1986–87 was ranked 89th in the world. Most World Amateur Champions have turned professional, but Terry Parsons (Wales), who won in 1982 aged 47, has remained amateur, and Paul Mifsud, who won in 1985 aged 38, and retained his title in 1986, had already tried being a professional, returning to the amateur ranks after reaching 49th in the rankings.

One indication of the spread of snooker around the world is that players from 23 nations were involved in the World Amateur Championships in 1985: England, Wales, Scotland, the Republic of Ireland, Northern Ireland, Malta, Australia, New Zealand, Egypt, Belgium, Sweden, Mauritius, Thailand, India, Singapore, Pakistan, Zimbabwe, Sri Lanka, Isle of Man, Hong Kong, Canada, Kenya and Iceland. In 1984 there were two players from the US.

World Champions. Jimmy White, the 1980 World Amateur Champion, a title he won aged 18, with the World Professional Champion of that year, Cliff Thorburn.

The professional game has made little impact on these countries, mostly because the professional circuit is based in Great Britain. In 1984, the WPBSA decided to improve their system of admitting new professionals (which then involved a sub-committee for considering applications) by recognizing a series of professional ticket events (amateur tournaments played at holiday camps), from which players could qualify for membership. The bias was still heavily in favour of British players because of the choice of venues, but the system was more democratic than it had been before.

In Australia, professionalism has long been a part of the game, for snooker was probably introduced in the late 1880s by an English professional, Frank Smith senior, who had learned the game from John Roberts junior. At the turn of the century, billiards, the older game was dominated by the Lindrum family – Fred, Fred junior, Walter and Horace. The youngest, Horace, was the best snooker player of the Lindrums, appearing in his first World Championship final in 1936, and becoming the only Austra-

Terry Griffiths with the Fred Pontin Challenge Cup in 1981. Griffiths was one of the professionals regularly to play the holiday camp circuit.

Pontins Holiday Camp at Prestatyn, Wales, has been a top venue for competitive amateur players for many years. As can be seen, the facilities in the main snooker hall are excellent.

lian to win it in 1952, when it was devalued by the withdrawal of all the British players. Warren Simpson and Eddie Charlton were the first modern Australians to reach the top ranks of the game. In 1970 the World Championship was held in Australia, and Warren Simpson, surprisingly, reached the final to lose to John Spencer. Since then Eddie Charlton has been their leading player, reaching the world final three times, losing to John Pulman, and to Ray Reardon twice.

The Winfield Masters, played in a Sydney television studio (like BBC's *Pot Black*), changed its format in 1983 to one of longer matches in a knockout format, giving Australia a taste of the British circuit tournament. A WPBSA subsidy helped to put the Australian Professional Championship on a sound footing in 1985 when Eddie Charlton, who, except for one year, had been champion since 1964, was beaten in the final 10-7 by John Campbell.

Snooker has also appeared on Canadian television, but not always successfully. Although Canadian snooker developed in the shadow of pool, there were outstanding players before the Second World War, principally Con Stanbury and George Chenier. In the 1970s, following the British revival, snooker gained ground in Canada. The Canadian Open was inaugurated in 1974 at the National Exhibition Centre in Toronto, and in its seven-year existence was won by Cliff Thorburn (four times), Alex Higgins (twice), and John Spencer. In 1977, when the tournament was held in a marquee, dripping rainwater and flies were among the distractions for the players, while the event itself had to compete with fairs, circus events, and noisy music. The first Canadian television broadcast was of the 1980 Open (ironically the last), but the lighting was primitive, and the winner, World Champion Thorburn, remained better known in Britain than his native Canada.

Canadian professional championships were instituted in 1983 and benefited from a WPBSA subsidy in 1985, when Cliff Thorburn, not surprisingly, was champion. At the end of the year a new tournament, the BCE Canadian Masters, was staged in the Canadian Broadcasting Corporation's television studios. The television coverage was the best so far in Canada, and the games were good, too, with Dennis Taylor beating Steve Davis in the final. Steve Davis beat Willie Thorne in 1986.

BCE also sponsored a pioneering tournament in Belgium – the BCE Belgian Classic. The event took place in the casino at Ostend, and was not only the first professional tournament to be promoted on the continent, but was also given nine hours of Belgian television time and earned good ratings. Terry Griffiths won the inaugural event. During the tournament some of the Barry Hearn Matchroom players, who are closely associated with the manufacturers of Riley tables, the main rivals of BCE, played an exhibition in a Riley club at Bruges, about 20 kilometres away. Some of the players in the Classic complained, but no WPBSA rules had been broken as the regulations barring players from performing within 50 miles of a tournament was not in operation for this event. However, as the 1986–87 season progressed Hearn let it be known that his players would not take part in the 1987 Bruges event due to a clash of dates with the new Rothmans Matchroom League. Although hasty arrangements were made by the WPBSA to present a credible field for Bruges, in February it was announced that the tournament had to be cancelled. Without so many of the top players, the television coverage was to be cut from seven days to two, and the interest of potential sponsors waned. The cancellation of the event was a 'victory' for Hearn, who had proved that overseas development of the game relied much more on his talents than on the WPBSA promotions department.

The success of the Belgian event on television in 1986 was not surprising since some areas in Belgium and Holland can pick up BBC transmissions, and they already had the nucleus of a snooker-watching audience. They clearly recognized that they were due to get second best in 1987.

The biggest promotional work in snooker in recent years has been taking place in the Far East, under the aegis of Barry Hearn. Hearn began by taking Steve Davis and Tony Meo on exhibition tours, and in 1983 he also took Doug Mountjoy and Terry Griffiths, the four of them joining up with Cheung Che-Ming, the Hong Kong Champion, and Stanley Leung in a new tournament, the Camus Hong Kong Masters. Mountjoy won. The same tourists took part in a similar event in Thailand, the Bangkok Golden Cue, won by Meo, who also won a Masters tournament shown on Thai television.

Thailand is a rapidly growing snooker stronghold – the people had seen British snooker on television, and the 1983 tournament was watched by about 25 million, more than half the population, and a bigger audience than British television can command. Thailand had its first player in the World Amateur Championship that same year, and two years later

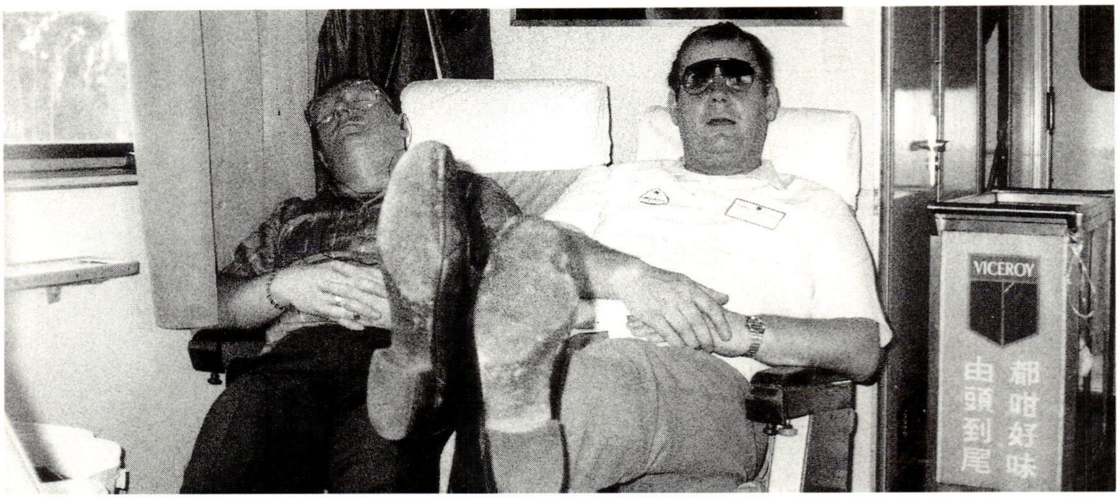

The joys of touring the Far East. Dennis Taylor and referee Len Ganley take a nap, probably the safest thing to do if you cannot read the signs.

its first professional, Sakchair Simngam, who played in the Rest of the World side in the 1986 Car Care Plan World Cup.

The Hearn group have recently extended their regular Eastern trips to take in Singapore, Malaysia, Dubai, Bahrain and China. Hearn is fond of pointing out that 90 per cent of the world's population does not yet know about snooker, and is waiting to be exploited. The Far Eastern tournaments are not promoted by the WPBSA, but with the exhibitions and appearances, are very much Hearn promotional exercises, with Riley tables, Goya 'Matchroom' toiletries, Cathay Pacific and Camus (cognac) being well to the fore. As the Far Eastern market booms, so hundreds of Riley tables are distributed. Hearn is a director of Rileys and Steve Davis has an interest in each table sold. As an incentive to buy, each club ordering a table was entitled to an exhibition match.

At the end of 1986, two of Barry Hearn's players, Dennis Taylor and Tony Meo, gave exhibitions in Tokyo's first snooker club, in Kukuchi's fashion emporium. The experiment was so successful that a number of Riley tables were exported, with Hearn promising more tours after the British season. In February 1987, Hearn announced a big new £100,000 tournament in Peking, China, with television coverage expecting to reach an enormous 1,000 million viewers. British American Tobacco were sponsoring the event, whose dates ironically overlapped those scheduled for the ill-fated Belgian Classic.

The United States, where pool is very firmly established, is a market which has so far defied snooker. Jim Rempe, the world's best pool player, is a WPBSA professional, and took part in two ranking tournaments in 1985, to earn a world ranking of 110th. Rempe and Mike Sigel played Davis and Griffiths in a challenge in which each player played his two opponents at both snooker and pool. Not surprisingly, the British players won the snooker matches and the Americans the pool matches. The event was at Dallas, but the presence of the world's best snooker players did not seem to impress America.

Leading players in Toronto for the BCE Canadian Masters. Left to right: Joe Johnson, Willie Thorne, Alex Higgins, Jimmy White, Dennis Taylor, Steve Davis, Tony Knowles and Cliff Thorburn. Davis' suit was at the cleaners.

THE PROFESSIONAL CIRCUIT

Although the preliminary rounds of the BCE International were played early in September 1986, and those of the Rothmans Grand Prix were held at the same time, it was the Langs Scottish Masters that really got the 1986–87 professional snooker season under way on 18 September, just as it had each season since 1981–82. This Glasgow tournament began life at the Kelvin Hall, but moved after one year to the Holiday Inn, and from 1984 has been held at the Hospitality Inn. The history of the competition goes back to the time when the Friends of Maccabi, a Scottish charity, promoted an exhibition match between Steve Davis and Alex Higgins. The whisky manufacturers Langs stepped in to sponsor this exhibition and its success led to the current tournament. Television coverage comes from BBC Scotland, and prize money has risen from £20,500 in 1981, to £40,000 in 1986–87. The entry is restricted to eight invited players, one of whom is always Scottish. Jimmy White won the inaugural tournament, then Steve Davis won three consecutive titles. Cliff Thorburn then won the event in 1985 and 1986.

A new event in 1986–87, the Matchroom Professional Championship, took place at the same time as the Langs Scottish Masters. It was a tournament specially arranged for the Matchroom professionals under the management of Barry Hearn. At the time there were seven, but the newest signing, Jimmy White, was already committed to the Langs, so there were six entrants. The prize money, at £100,000, was much greater than the Langs, and each player was guaranteed at least £5,000. The venue was the Cliffs Pavilion, at Southend, and there was no television coverage. Willie Thorne won the £50,000 first prize by taking the last three frames against Steve Davis, who had to be content with winnings of £20,000.

By the time these two events had taken place, the early rounds of the first open tournament, which in 1986–87 was called the BCE International, had taken place at the Assembly Rooms, Derby. The 16 players remaining fought out the televised phase of the tournament, over the fortnight at the end of September and beginning of October.

This event started life as the Jameson International in 1981. It was promoted by Mike Watterson, and sponsored by Irish Distillers to get the brand name of Jameson Whiskey known outside Ireland. The television exposure was on ITV, and in the first year ran to nearly 11 hours. The prize money was £66,500. The Jameson International was the first tournament outside the World Championship for which world ranking points were at stake.

The first two Jameson tournaments held their final stages at the Assembly Rooms, Derby, but in 1983 it moved to a new venue, the Eldon Square Leisure Centre, Newcastle. In 1985 the WPBSA had its own television contract with ITV, effectively taking over from Watterson as promoter, and Jameson withdrew their sponsorship, well satisfied with its success. Meanwhile, Barry Hearn's Matchroom group was endorsing Goya's range of men's toilet requisites, and Goya decided to sponsor what now became known as the Goya Matchroom Trophy, at another venue, the Trentham Gardens, Stoke. The television coverage rose to 32 hours, and the prize money was raised to its current level of £175,000. While Steve Davis, the first of the Matchroom players, had won the Jameson in three of its four years (Knowles won the other), ironically it was the non-Matchroom player Cliff Thorburn who won the Goya. When Goya withdrew after only one year, BCE – the tables and equipment manufacturer – took up the sponsorship for 1986, and the tournament now became the BCE International. The first tournament under this name provided Neal Foulds with his first major victory, when he beat Cliff Thorburn in the final.

After the BCE International, the players spent ten days in preliminary rounds, trying to qualify for the Tennents UK Open at the Coral Snooker Club, Bootle, and then the Hofmeister World Doubles at Romily Forum, Stockport. On 18 October, the survivors (i.e. the last 32) of the preliminary rounds of the Rothmans Grand Prix arrived at the Hexagon, Reading, for the second ranking tournament of the season.

The Rothmans arose out of the Professional Players Tournament, first staged in 1982 by the WPBSA to pass on to the players, rather than the tax man, the sums it was making from television. It was unique in that it was meant to lose money and not make it. Ranking points were at stake in a tournament held at two venues: the International Snooker Club, Aston, and La Reserve, Sutton Coldfield. Ray Reardon won the tournament, his first big success for nearly four years. In 1983 the event moved to the Redwood Lodge Country Club, Bristol, and was very successful. When the sponsorship of State Express for the World Team Championship came to an end, it was thought that the Professional Players Tournament should replace the team event in its television slot. Thus the BBC took over televising it, and Rothmans stepped in to become sponsors. The

Neal Foulds with the BCE International, his first major trophy, which he won in 1986. With him is his father Geoff, also a professional.

The Preston Guild Hall, home of the UK Championship, sponsored for many years by Coral, but taken over in 1986 by Tennents.

World Team Championship venue of the Hexagon, Reading, was also taken over, and the event became the Rothmans Grand Prix.

In 1984, 37 hours of television time was given to the tournament, which quickly rose to well over 40 hours. The £32,000 prize money, which the WPBSA handed out in 1982, had risen to £275,000 in 1986–87. Jimmy White took the £55,000 first prize (as well as the £5,500 for the highest televised break), and Rex Williams had his best pay day of £33,000 as runner-up.

At this stage in the season of 1985–86 and 1986–87, eight invited players flew to Toronto for the BCE Canadian Masters. For the Rothmans finalists it has almost been a case of leaving the table at Reading and dashing for the plane. Jimmy White and Steve Davis won the first two tournaments.

Meanwhile, in November 1986, the preliminary rounds of the Dulux British Open were held at the Conference Centre, Solihull, followed by the preliminary rounds of the Mercantile Credit Classic at the Norbreck Castle Hotel, Blackpool. On 14 November 1986, the 64 remaining contestants in the Tennents UK Open arrived at the Guild Hall, Preston, for the next ranking tournament of the season. This old-established tournament was promoted by Mike Watterson in 1977 as the UK Professional Championship, and was held at the Tower Circus, Blackpool. The snooker ball manufacturers Super Crystalate sponsored the event, which was not a great success. However, Coral, the bookmakers, had been anxious to sponsor snooker, and they took over the sponsorship in 1978, when the event moved to a new venue, the Guild Hall, Preston, where it has since remained. The WPBSA took over the promotion of the event from Watterson in 1983, and in 1984 the event became open, with ranking points attached. Coral withdrew their sponsorship in 1985, but a sister company, Tennents, took over.

A feature of this Tournament is that no match is less than the best of 17 frames. Television coverage has extended from around ten to nearly 50 hours, and the prize money has risen from £7,000 to £300,000. The winner in 1986, Steve Davis, collected £60,000 of this total.

In 1986–87, the players headed straight from Preston to the Derngate Centre, Northampton, for the Hofmeister World Doubles Championship. This championship has remained unchanged since its inception in 1982, except for its venue, which for the first year only was Crystal Palace. Steve Davis and Tony Meo have won this championship every year except one. The promoters are Sports Sponsorship International, and ITV has televised it from the beginning, now more than doubling the initial allowance of 14 hours. The prize money too has crept up, from £66,000 to £200,000.

Semi-finalists in the 1985 Hofmeister World Doubles Championship, Willie Thorne and Cliff Thorburn, with the eventual winners Steve Davis and Tony Meo.

World Champions who came together in Nottingham in 1985 for the Kit Kat Break for World Champions. From left: Fred Davis, John Pulman, John Spencer, Ray Reardon, Alex Higgins, Terry Griffiths, Cliff Thorburn, Steve Davis and Dennis Taylor.

The first finals of 1987 were for the Mercantile Credit Classic at Norbreck Castle, Blackpool. This ranking tournament began life in 1979 as the Wilsons Classic (since the Granada television coverage only reached the Lancashire area the competition was sponsored by the Lancashire brewers, Wilsons). It was an eight-man, two-day event, and the promoter was Barwell Sports. However, when the television area taking the event widened in 1981, Wilsons withdrew and Lada, the car manufacturers, stepped in at the last minute. In 1983 the tournament received full ITV network coverage, and in 1984 the WPBSA took over the promotion, and Mercantile Credit the sponsorship.

Now the tournament is an open one, television coverage has increased from three hours, in 1982, to around 30 hours. In the same time the prize money has increased from £15,000 to £250,000. Steve Davis collected £50,000 of it in 1986–87, beating Jimmy White 13-12 in the final, White's consolation prize being £30,000, plus £5,000 for the highest televized break, a prize he was making a habit of claiming in 1986-87.

On 26 January 1987 the top 16 players in the world took part in the Benson and Hedges Masters at the Wembley Conference Centre. This event, sponsored by the cigarette giant Gallaher, whose Park Drive brand had been associated with early 1970s World Championships, has been promoted by Benson and Hedges since 1975, making them snooker's longest continuous sponsors. It was originally held at West Centre Hotel, Fulham, and then went in 1976 to the New London Theatre, a theatre-in-the-round. In 1979 the tournament moved to its present venue at the Wembley Conference Centre. The BBC television coverage has risen from three or four hours to 36 in 1986, while the prize money has increased from £5,000 in 1975, to £175,000 in 1986.

From 15 February 1987, the final phases of the Dulux British Open were held at the Assembly Rooms, Derby. This tournament was first promoted by Mike Watterson as the British Gold Cup in 1980, and found a sponsor in 1981 when it became the Yamaha Organs Trophy, which was networked by ITV, breaking new ground in their treatment of snooker. The venue was the Assembly Rooms, Derby. This tournament became the Yamaha International Masters, and was played in mini-leagues, giving audiences a chance to see four players in one session. From each group emerged semi-final groups, from which two players won through to a final.

When the Yamaha contract expired in 1985, and the WPBSA took over the promotion, Dulux (the paint company) became the sponsors, and the event was given the status of an open ranking tournament. Apart from the venue of the Assembly Rooms, there is little relation between the old Yamaha and the new Dulux. The seven hours which ITV devoted to the 1981 Yamaha had grown to 31 hours for the 1986 Dulux, and the prize money had increased tenfold from £30,000 to £300,000 in 1987. The first Dulux Open was won by Silvino Francisco in 1985, in his controversial final with Kirk Stevens.

The Bournemouth International Centre was booked for 18-21 March 1987 for the World Team Cup, although Car Care Plan, the sponsors in 1986, had announced that they were not renewing their sponsorship. The World Cup began in 1979 as the State Express World Cup, which later became the World Team Classic. The sponsors were British American Tobacco, the prize money was a reasonable £27,500, the BBC covered it on television, and the event was very successful. Wales won.

The first two competitions were in Birmingham and London, but when the event moved to the Hexagon, Reading, in 1981, it became even more successful. When the State Express sponsorship contract ended in 1983, the WPBSA moved the Rothmans Grand Prix into the World Cup television spot. The World Team championship was not held in 1984, but was revived in its current spot in 1985, promoted by Mike Watterson and sponsored by Guinness. The venue was the Conference Centre, Bournemouth, and BBC televised each day's play. Guinness' sponsorship lasted only one year, and Car Care Plan took over for 1986.

The Assembly Rooms, Derby during the Dulux British Open. The first ITV networked snooker was televised from here.

Ireland, represented by Eugene Hughes, Alex Higgins and Dennis Taylor, winners of the Guinness World Cup in 1985, a victory they were to repeat in the following two years.

In 1984, the WPBSA decided that the country which won the title could enter a 'B' team the following year. Since this meant England fielded a second side in 1985 which contained two board members in John Spencer and Willie Thorne, it was humorously called, after the Rest of the World team, 'the Rest of the Board'. In 1986, Ireland had the 'B' team which, not surprisingly, failed to win a frame. Silvino Francisco, having a dispute with the board, was omitted from the Rest of the World team, which also failed to win a frame.

The biggest joke were the original plans for 1987, in which the board decreed that nationality would not now be the basis for choosing the World Cup teams. Instead, the No.1 ranked player in the world would team up with Nos.16 and 17, the No.2 ranked player with Nos.15 and 18, and so on, with Nos. 8, 9, and 24 making the eighth team of three. There seemed no particular reason for this. It meant that three members of the WPBSA board, Rex Williams, John Virgo and David Taylor, would all play, as would all seven of Barry Hearn's Matchroom players, so perhaps they were happy with the system.

Luckily, after much criticism in the press, common sense prevailed, and the tournament went ahead on the normal country-by-country basis. Tuborg stepped in at the last moment as sponsors. Ireland 'A', in the persons of

Jimmy White and Alex Higgins before a World Championship match at the Crucible. They played a tremendous semi-final in 1982.

A view of the World Championships at the Crucible which the televiewer does not get. Scorers, commentators, television cameras are all at one end, the public at the other. Dennis Taylor and Cliff Thorburn are in play on the two tables.

captain Dennis Taylor, Alex Higgins and Eugene Hughes, won for the third successive year.

The number of televised hours, which had reached a high of nearly 37 in 1983, dropped to seven in 1986 but revived to about 11 in 1987. This event provided some variety in snooker television coverage, and it is to be hoped that the WPBSA do not manage to kill it.

The Benson and Hedges Irish Masters, scheduled for 24–29 March in 1987, for the Goffs sales ring, Kill, County Kildare, has been a regular feature on the circuit since 1978, promoted by Benson and Hedges Ireland. It is restricted to 12 invited players, who shared £75,000 in 1986.

The last event on the circuit, the Embassy World Professional Championship, has a non-televised qualifying

Left: Goffs Sales Ring, at Kill in County Kildare, makes a natural arena for snooker. It is the home of the Benson & Hedges Irish Masters.

Below: Jimmy White, the 1985 Benson & Hedges Irish Masters winner, with the beaten finalist, Alex Higgins.

Light relief at the Crucible. Ray Reardon dons a beard to play an exhibition match with John Virgo to fill a gap caused by a match finishing early.

phase of nearly a fortnight. It begins in the last week of March at the Guild Hall, Preston. Television coverage commences at the last 32-player stage at the Crucible Theatre, Sheffield, beginning about the middle of April and extending to the first Sunday (or Monday) in May.

The World Championship was instituted in 1927, and its progress is closely allied to the history of the game as a whole, as outlined in the first chapter. Embassy (a cigarette brand of W.D. and H.O. Wills) became the sponsors in 1976, when the tournament was not very well promoted by 'Q' Promotions. Embassy maintained their sponsorship in 1977, when Mike Watterson promoted the tournament from the Crucible, Sheffield, and the event has not looked back since. In view of the enormous success

The Crucible set up for the world semi-final in 1984. Jimmy White sits ready to begin while referee Jim Thorpe has spotted the balls and awaits the entrance of Kirk Stevens.

of snooker/television/sponsorship since then, it is remarkable to think that there was no sponsor in 1975. The championship has remained at the Crucible, an ideal venue for snooker, and since 1984 has been promoted by the WPBSA.

The final of the Embassy World Professional Championship is now one of the big sporting and television spectaculars of the year, and luckily the 1985 and 1986 finals were exciting affairs which fulfilled all expectations. Viewing figures in Britain match those for any other sport.

During the 1980s, the hours the BBC devoted to the championship increased every year from 53 in 1980 to nearly 119 in 1986. The value of the championship in prize money has risen even more steeply. In 1973, when the championship was drawn together at one venue (Manchester), the prize money was £8,000. In 1976, Embassy's first year, it was £15,300. In 1979, when Terry Griffiths took the first prize of £10,000, it was £35,000. In 1980 it was £60,000. It has since risen in leaps and bounds until, in 1987, it was £400,000.

After the Embassy, snooker players either go on tour or on holiday, fulfil their commitments in respect of appearances, exhibition matches, and so on, and four months later begin preparing for the next season's round.

The World Champion, 1986. Joe Johnson with the champagne and with one hand on the cup, which wife Terryll thinks deserves both hands.

TODAY'S LEADING PLAYERS

John Campbell

Born: 10 April 1953, Australia
Professional: 1982
Ranking, 1983–87: 39, 28, 31, 18, 22
Best Performance: Australian Professional Champion, 1985

John Campbell was Australian amateur champion in 1979 and finalist in 1974 and 1981. He beat Eddie Charlton 10-7 in the Australian Professional Championship of 1985.

Eddie Charlton

Born: 31 October 1929, Australia
Professional: 1960
Ranking, 1983–87: 6, 6, 12, 25, 26
Best Performances: World Professional Championship finalist 1973, 1975, semi-finalist 1970, 1972, 1978, 1979, 1982

Eddie Charlton has been a fixture on the Australian and indeed, world snooker scene for over 20 years. He won the Australian Professional Championship in 1964 and, until he lost it in 1985, had held it continuously except for 1968. In the World Championship he lost his two finals to Ray Reardon, one by 31-30, having led 29-23. Charlton has been unlucky on the big occasions, losing many matches by a narrow margin.

He regularly visits Britain for the big tournaments, and was a *Pot Black* regular. Eddie believes in centre-ball striking, and is not a great fan of side. He earned the nickname 'Steady Eddie' and was always thereabouts without winning. A very keen sportsman, he practised athletics, surfing, cricket, tennis and boxing, and a proud moment was to carry the Olympic torch on one of its stages for the 1956 Melbourne Games.

Fred Davis

Born: 14 August 1913, England
Professional: 1930
Ranking, 1983–87: 28, 46, 56, 47, 62
Best Performances: World Professional Champion 1948, 1949, 1951, finalist 1940, 1947, 1950, 1964, 1965, 1966; Professional Match-Play Champion 1952, 1953, 1954, 1955, 1956

That Fred Davis should be ranked 47th in the competitive world of snooker when well into his 70s is a sporting achievement which does not receive the recognition it deserves. He has even overcome short-sightedness. Fred has always been overshadowed by his brother Joe, the world champion for 20 years. He finally won the world title in 1948, when 35 years old. In 1980 he won the world billiards title – only he and his brother Joe have won both titles.

For a while Fred more or less gave up his 'world' title from 1957, when the game was in a slump, and then enjoyed a second career in the television boom time. His courtly manner and the twinkle in his eye made him a favourite with the viewers.

One of the most familiar figures on the circuit, Australian Eddie Charlton has been ever-present during snooker's boom.

Steve Davis

Born: 22 August 1957, England
Professional: 1978
Ranking, 1983–87: 1, 1, 1, 1, 1
Best Performances: World Professional Champion 1981, 1983, 1984, 1987, finalist 1985, 1986; Coral UK Champion 1980, 1984, 1985; Yamaha Masters Champion 1981, 1982; Jameson International Champion 1981, 1983, 1984; Benson and Hedges Masters Champion 1982; Langs Scottish Masters Champion 1982, 1983, 1984; Lada Classic Champion 1983, 1984; Benson and Hedges Irish Masters Champion 1983, 1984; Rothmans Grand Prix Champion 1985; Dulux British Open Champion 1986; Tennents UK Open Champion 1986; Mercantile Credit Classic Champion 1987

Steve Davis, with his manager Barry Hearn behind him like a Svengali, has made himself into an almost perfect snooker-playing machine. At one time, after he had broken through by winning the 1981 World Championship, he looked likely to dominate the game. Luckily for snooker, chinks appeared in his armour, and while he remained easily the best player in the world, he suffered some major reversals.

His strengths are a perfect cueing action, and a feel for the game's tactics which allows him to pick unerringly the best shot for the occasion. He is devoted to snooker and jealously guards his No.1 ranking. He plays better in televised tournaments, and in tournaments which carry ranking points.

This single-mindedness – which in his early days seemed to be alleviated only by a passion for playing space invaders – and a certainty in his skill, has perhaps prevented him becoming popular with the casual spectator. There is a feeling that his character has been moulded by Hearn, and that he can relate only to snooker and its commercial possibilities. He is a great sportsman and behaves impeccably – perhaps he needs a suspicion of a tantrum to get more fans on his side.

Above left: Fred Davis in 1979. For a man from the era of his brother Joe, whom he almost got onto even terms with around the time of the Second World War, to be ranked as low as 47 in 1986–87 is astonishing.

Above: The world's leading player, Steve Davis, with the World Championship trophy he won four times in the 1980s.

Tony Drago

Born: 22 September 1965, Malta
Professional: 1985
Ranking, 1983–87: —, —, —, 37, 31

Tony Drago's rapid potting has won him many fans. A quarter-final defeat by Steve Davis in the Tennents UK Open in 1986, when he rushed a yellow and missed to lose 9-8, suggested that all he needed to spring up the rankings was a little steadiness.

Steve Duggan

Born: 10 April 1958, England
Professional: 1983
Ranking, 1983–87: —, 55, 70, 35, 37

Duggan's best run was the Goya Matchroom Trophy in 1985, when he beat ex-World Champions Fred Davis and Ray Reardon, before losing in the quarter-final to another ex-world Champion, the eventual winner — Canadian Cliff Thorburn.

Tony Drago, from Malta, is one of the fastest potters in the game and could be one of the fastest up the ladder of success.

Ray Edmonds

Born: 28 May 1936, England
Professional: 1978
Ranking, 1983–87: 34, 49, 51, 46, 60

Despite being World Amateur Champion in 1972 and 1974, and World Billiards Champion in 1985, he has not yet reached a major professional snooker final.

Patsy Fagan

Born: 15 January 1951, Republic of Ireland
Professional: 1976
Ranking, 1983–87: 26, 37, 33, 42, 76
Best Performance: Super Crystalate UK Champion 1977

Patsy Fagan looked like a future World Champion when he won the UK Championship in his first year as a professional, but he lost confidence, particularly with the rest. If he could regain his old flair, he could advance up the rankings again.

Neal Foulds

Born: 13 July 1963, England
Professional: 1983
Ranking, 1983–87: —, 30, 23, 13, 3
Best Performances: World Professional Championship semi-finalist 1987; BCE International Champion 1986; Tennents UK Open finalist 1986; Dulux British Open finalist 1987

Neal Foulds was coached by his father Geoff, also a professional (ranked No.79 in 1986–87). They were the first father and son to compete in a major tournament together. Foulds wears contact lenses. He is an excellent all-round player who, after progressing steadily in the rankings, made a breakthrough in the 1986–87 season, winning his first major tournament and advancing to third.

Neal Foulds, in action against Tony Knowles, was the most improved player on the circuit in 1986–87 and seemed destined for a long run as one of the game's regular winners.

Above: Silvino Francisco, whose first major title came in 1985, and whose direct style bothers all the best players.

Right: Peter Francisco practising. From a famous snooker-playing South African family, he has the background to resist the pressures of life at the top.

Danny Fowler

Born: 30 July 1956, England
Professional: 1984
Ranking, 1983–87: —, —, 55, 33, 40

Danny Fowler reached the Crucible stage (the last 32) of the World Championship in his second season as a professional in 1986.

Peter Francisco

Born: 14 February 1962, South Africa
Professional: 1984
Ranking, 1983–87: —, —, 59, 26, 18
Best Performance: BCE International semi-finalist 1986

Peter Francisco comes from a famous family of players. Father Mannie was a world amateur championship finalist (at snooker and billiards), while uncle Silvino is ranked No.10 in the world. Peter looks to have the skill and temperament to follow his uncle into the world's top dozen.

Silvino Francisco

Born: 3 May 1946, South Africa
Professional: 1978
Ranking, 1983–87: 21, 17, 13, 12, 10
Best Performance: Dulux British Open Champion 1985

Silvino Francisco has made steady progress in the rankings, but unfortunately his first major win, the Dulux British Open in 1985, was marred by his brush with Kirk Stevens, whom he accused of taking drugs. The long-drawn-out disciplinary struggle with the WPBSA which ensued, and which led Francisco to sue for libel, has affected his form a little.

Terry Griffiths

Born: 16 October 1947, Wales
Professional: 1978
Ranking, 1983–87: 9, 8, 8, 10, 6
Best Performances: Embassy World Professional Champion 1979; Benson and Hedges Masters Champion 1980; Benson and Hedges Irish Masters Champion 1980, 1982; Lada Classic Champion 1982; Coral UK Champion 1982

Terry Griffiths won the World Championship in his first season as a professional in 1978–79, and when Steve Davis emerged as the world's leading player in 1981, Griffiths for a while was his main challenger. Since 1982 he has played well without recapturing the fluency of those days. The boyish charm of his championship year has been replaced with a care-worn expression and a tendency to fiddle indecisively on his shots.

Griffiths joined the Barry Hearn stable in 1982 and seems to be the player least in harmony with the Hearn ideal. He is an intelligent student of the game, but does not think that snooker and its commercialization is the main reason for living. He likes a private life. He is sporting in defeat, and perhaps his main barrier to another World Championship is a slight lack of dedication.

Below left: Griffiths looks tired in this shot, and since the hectic year following his World Championship has usually looked as if he enjoyed the game more before he was forced into the competitiveness of the top flight.

Below: Terry Griffiths in play. His 1979 World Championship victory was one of the highlights of modern snooker, but he has had difficulty keeping a place in the top eight.

Mike Hallett

Born: 6 July 1959, England
Professional: 1979
Ranking, 1983–87: 32, 25, 28, 27, 16
Best Performance: Embassy World Professional quarter-finalist 1987

Mike Hallett occasionally plays brilliant matches, as defeats of Steve Davis and Dennis Taylor (in the World Championship) indicate, but he has not yet sustained his effort throughout a tournament. He played well with Stephen Hendry to reach the final of the Hofmeister World Doubles in 1986, which might inspire him to more sustained spells of form. In the 1986 World Championship he eliminated the holder, Dennis Taylor, in the first round.

Stephen Hendry

Born: 13 January 1969, Scotland
Professional: 1985
Ranking, 1983–87: —, —, —, 51, 23
Best Performance: Embassy World Professional quarter-finalist 1987

Stephen Hendry was not quite 18 years old when he made a big impression in the 1986–87 season. First, in the third round of the Tennents UK Open, Alex Higgins had to take the last three frames to beat him 9-8, then he reached the final of the Hofmeister World Doubles with Mike Hallett, and in the next tournament he reached the semi-final of the Mercantile Credit Classic before losing to Steve Davis. If he maintains this progress he should be in the top eight by 1990.

The suit looks out of place on the youthful Stephen Hendry. Nothing looks out of place when he gets on the table, for he plays like a veteran.

Above left: A typical Alex Higgins pose. Getting rid of his tie and playing to the gallery with some remark or other.

Above: Alex Higgins in another of his typical stances, studying the balls and thinking hard about his next shot.

Alex Higgins

Born: 18 March 1949, N. Ireland
Professional: 1971
Ranking, 1983–87: 5, 9, 9, 6, 9
Best Performances: World Professional Champion 1972, 1982, finalist 1976, 1980; Benson and Hedges Masters Champion 1978, 1981, 1987; Coral UK Champion 1983

Higgins is the bad boy of the snooker circuit, whose dazzling displays alternate with irrational and scandalous behaviour. Developing his game in Belfast, he came to England and won the World Professional Championship at his first attempt, playing in an inspirational style that earned the nickname 'Hurricane'. His method of playing, full of twitches and mannerisms, is very expressive, and his nervous involvement in a match, whether at the table or watching his opponent, gets the audience on his side. When he is fired up, and the audience is behind him, he can manufacture breaks of breathtaking brilliance. He calls himself, not without justification, 'the people's champion'.

Higgins' volatile behaviour behind the scenes and at home has kept the tabloid newspapers full of spicy stories. The most serious incident, from a snooker point of view, was still unresolved as the 1986–87 season progressed. During the Tennents UK Open, Higgins was escorted from the Guild Hall, Preston, by police after allegations that he had head-butted the tournament director, Paul Hatherell. It was the latest of several disciplinary scrapes with the WPBSA, one of which prevented him being ranked and cost him a suspension for five tournaments as well as a record £12,000 fine.

His marital ups and downs were equally well publicized, and affected his performances at the table. The big tearful scene with his wife and baby at the end of the 1982 World Championship success contrasted with periods of depression, when he hardly seemed interested in the game. There were divorce proceedings, drug stories, violence, suicide talk – everything the tabloid press deals in, Higgins seemed to provide.

Despite all this, Higgins lives for snooker as a great painter lives for his art, and is the most exciting player of all.

Joe Johnson winning his title. The ease with which he deals with the media makes it difficult to understand why success on television was so long coming.

Eugene Hughes

Born: 4 November 1955, Republic of Ireland
Professional: 1981
Ranking, 1983–87: 35, 27, 21, 20, 24
Best Performance: BCE International semi-finalist 1986

Eugene Hughes plays a steady game and is advancing slowly up the rankings. His biggest successes were as a member of the Irish team which won the World Cup in 1985, 1986 and 1987.

Joe Johnson

Born: 29 July 1952, England
Professional: 1979
Ranking, 1983–87: 23, 19, 16, 8, 5
Best Performances: Embassy World Professional Champion 1986, finalist 1987; Professional Players Tournament finalist 1983

Joe Johnson was commonly regarded as a sound player who would not reach the top because nerves afflicted him when he played on television. All this seemed very strange when he sailed through the 1986 World Professional Championship in relaxed style to pull off a 150-1 surprise by taking the title. The public took to him immediately – with his two-tone 'lucky' shoes, happy home life, numerous children, modesty and obvious joy in his achievement, he represented the ordinary man realizing a sporting dream, rather than a man on the brink of fame and fortune. It transpired that his main love is singing, and his ambition is to get to the top of the pop charts (he was rehearsing with his band when surprised for the *This Is Your Life* television programme).

He reached the final again in 1987 — 'It's like a dream,' he said — and increased his popularity.

Warren King

Born: 1 April 1955, Australia
Professional: 1982
Ranking, 1983–87: —, 48, 35, 41, 39

Warren King twice won the Australian Amateur Championship, but has not yet passed the quarter-final stage in a major professional tournament.

Tony Knowles

Born: 13 June 1955, England
Professional: 1980
Ranking, 1983–87: 4, 2, 3, 4, 7
Best Performances: Embassy World Professional semi-finalist 1983, 1985, 1986; Jameson International Champion 1982; Professional Players Tournament Champion 1983

Tony Knowles won snooker fame overnight with a 10-1 defeat of champion Steve Davis in the first round of the 1982 World Professional Championship. Steady performances in the following season raised him to second place in the world rankings in 1983–84, from which he has since slowly dropped to seventh.

Tall, dark and good-looking, he did himself and the game no good by serialized revelations in the *Sun* of his sexual exploits. Although he was paid £25,000, he was fined £5,000 by the WPBSA, and it has been calculated that the articles cost him a further £250,000 in lost earnings.

Knowles, of course, has earned far more than this in the meantime, and outside the season enjoys the good life in the sun. Perhaps he lacks the application to get to the very top. He has the skill, but has three times failed in the World Championship at the semi-final stage. He needs an ounce of flair or imagination to convert his talent to the highest class.

Inset below: The striking looks of Tony Knowles did not go unnoticed by the fans, and for a period in the 1980s his activities off the table seemed about to submerge his performances on it.

Bottom: Knowles water-skiing – or attempting to. A useful games player, he represented snooker in the televised Superstars *series.*

Steve Longworth

Born: 27 July 1948, England
Professional: 1984
Ranking, 1983–87: —, —, 37, 31, 32

The English Amateur Champion when he turned professional in 1984, Longworth reached the last 16 of the 1987 World Championship, and has reached the top 32 in the world.

Murdo Macleod

Born: 14 January 1947, Scotland
Professional: 1981
Ranking, 1983–87: 27, 29, 26, 22, 30

Murdo Macleod reached 22 in the rankings before, in the 1987 World Championship, winning his first match on television. He has been Scottish Champion.

Perrie Mans

Born: 14 October 1940, South Africa
Professional: 1961
Ranking, 1983–87: 17, 24, 30, 36, 50
Best Performances: Embassy World Professional finalist 1978, semi-finalist 1976; Benson and Hedges Masters Champion 1979

Perrie Mans became well-known to snooker followers in *Pot Black*, where his colourful waistcoats and left-handed long potting singled him out. He reached the final of the World Professional Championship in 1978, when he was beaten by Reardon, but the succeeding boom and the influx of talented younger players saw him slip down the rankings from seventh place, in 1979–80, until when the 1986–87 season started he had dropped outside the top 32 for the first time.

Perrie Mans, left, before his World Championship final with Ray Reardon in 1978. He has not done so well in the 1980s.

The hat is 1930s gangster, but the carnation more Maurice Chevalier. Family man and snappy dresser Tony Meo.

Dave Martin

Born: 9 May 1948, England
Professional: 1981
Ranking, 1983–87: 29, 26, 29, 28, 27
Best Performance: Yamaha International Masters finalist 1984

Dave Martin reached the semi-final of the Jameson International in his first season, and the three-man final of the Yamaha International Masters in 1984, but he has not yet managed to climb above 26 in the world rankings.

Tony Meo

Born: 4 October 1959, England
Professional: 1979
Ranking, 1983–87: 15, 10, 10, 11, 20
Best Performance: Lada Classic finalist 1984

Tony Meo was a precocious young player who toured the snooker halls with his friend Jimmy White playing money matches. He became the second well-known professional in Barry Hearn's stable. A snappy dresser, with a snappy left-handed style, especially when clearing up the colours in a frame already won, he is popular on the circuit, but branded himself a born loser after many near-misses. He seemed to play better with partners, often being the dominant player when he and Steve Davis won the Hofmeister World Doubles championship four times. He was also a member of England's World Cup winning team in 1983. A first defeat of Davis in 11 meetings in the 1987 Tolly Cobold English Professional Championship, which he won, could herald a more successful spell.

Although left-handed, Meo plays with his right hand when using the rest.

Doug Mountjoy

Born: 8 June 1942, Wales
Professional: 1976
Ranking, 1983–87: 12, 15, 15, 14, 14
Best Performances: Embassy World Professional finalist 1981; Benson and Hedges Masters Champion 1977; Coral UK Champion 1978; Benson and Hedges Irish Masters Champion 1979.

Doug Mountjoy has been in the world's top 16 for many years. He won his first professional tournament, the Benson and Hedges Masters, in 1977. He has had a few ups and downs, and illness halted him for a while in 1980–81, but he has always managed to do enough to maintain his ranking.

One of the best of the younger players who will be disputing the number one spot in a few years' time is John Parrott, but he has yet to win a major tournament.

Steve Newbury

Born: 21 April 1956, Wales
Professional: 1984
Ranking, 1983–87: —, —, 34, 40, 45

Steve Newbury reached the last 16 of the Jameson International and Dulux British Open in his first season, beating Terry Griffiths in the latter, but slipped a few places in the following seasons.

Dene O'Kane

Born: 24 February 1963, New Zealand
Professional: 1984
Ranking, 1983–87: —, —, 32, 39, 35
Best Performance: Embassy World Professional quarter-finalist 1987.

Dene O'Kane reached the first 32 in the rankings in his first season. He reached the quarter-finals of the Dulux British Open, and the Crucible stage of the World Championship in 1985 and 1987.

John Parrott

Born: 11 May 1964, England
Professional: 1983
Ranking, 1983–87: —, 20, 18, 17, 13
Best Performance: Lada Classic semi-finalist 1980; Embassy World Professional quarter-finalist 1985; Tennents UK Open semi-finalist 1986

John Parrott looked a future World Champion when, in his first season (1983–84), he beat Mountjoy, Higgins, Knowles, and almost Davis in the Lada Classic, and beat Knowles again in the World Professional Championship, before losing by only 13-11 to Dennis Taylor. Next year he reached the quarter-final of the World Professional Championship, before losing a great match 13-12 to Ray Reardon. He has now secured a place in the top 16.

Ray Reardon, who has more than once had trouble with the lights, trying a shade. Nobody has won more modern World Championships than Ray's six in the 1970s.

Ray Reardon

Born: 8 October 1932, Wales
Professional: 1967
Ranking, 1983–87: 2, 5, 6, 15, 38
Best Performances: World Professional Champion 1970, 1973, 1974, 1975, 1976, 1978; finalist 1982; Benson and Hedges Masters Champion 1976; Professional Players Tournament Champion 1982; Yamaha International Masters Champion 1983

Six times World Professional Champion, Ray Reardon just lost his edge as snooker really boomed. Congratulating Terry Griffiths on his 1979 World Championship, Reardon promised that the title was only lent, but despite an appearance in the 1982 final, he has not looked like regaining it. He has tried playing in spectacles since his long potting was really letting him down.

Reardon was the dominant figure in snooker in the 1970s, and in the 1980s has enjoyed the status of a 'wily old campaigner'. However, he won only two important matches in the 1985–86 season, and began to slide very rapidly down the rankings. He has been a great worker for snooker, both as a player and member of the WPBSA board, and he is one of the most popular and respected figures in the game.

Dean Reynolds

Born: 11 January 1963, England
Professional: 1981
Ranking, 1983–87: 19, 22, 24, 29, 15
Best Performance: Mercantile Credit Classic semi-finalist 1987

Dean Reynolds reached the last 16 of the World Professional Championship at his first attempt in 1982, but has not looked like winning a tournament. A left-hander, he produced his best in 1987, perhaps feeling that his top 32 spot was threatened. He reached the semi-final of the Mercantile Credit Classic before losing 9-8 to Jimmy White and considerably improved his ranking.

John Spencer

Born: 18 September 1935, England
Professional: 1967
Ranking, 1983–87: 16, 13, 20, 34, 28
Best Performances: World Professional Champion 1969, 1970, 1977, finalist 1972; Norwich Union Open Champion 1973, 1974; Benson and Hedges Masters Champion 1975; Benson and Hedges Irish Masters Champion 1978; Holsten Lager International Champion 1979

John Spencer was just about the best player in the world around 1970, and continued to win important tournaments throughout that decade, including the World Championship for the third time in 1977. He began to slip from this peak in the 1980s, and in 1984–85 discovered that he was suffering from a serious eye condition which gave him double vision. He takes steroids daily to arrest the condition.

Kirk Stevens

Born: 17 August 1958, Canada
Professional: 1978
Ranking, 1983–87: 7, 4, 5, 9, 21
Best Performances: Embassy World Professional semi-finalist 1980, 1984; Dulux British Open finalist 1985

Stevens is a brilliant potter, whose career looked assured when he reached the semi-final of the World Professional Championship in 1980. In 1983–84 he and Jimmy White inspired each other in two tremendous matches: in the Benson and Hedges Masters semi-final, when Stevens made a televised 147 maximum break; and in the World Professional Championship semi-final. Unfortunately for Stevens, White won both matches.

His only major victory to date has come in the World Cup, which he helped Canada to win in 1982. In 1985, after losing the final of the Dulux British Open to Silvino Francisco, he was accused of drug-taking. Although denying he had used drugs in a tournament, he entered a Toronto clinic in an attempt to conquer his problem.

While he slipped down the rankings a little, he has the verve to come back.

David Taylor

Born: 29 July 1943, England
Professional: 1968
Ranking, 1983–87: 10, 16, 14, 21, 25
Best Performances: Embassy World Professional semi-finalist 1980; Coral UK finalist 1978; Yamaha International Masters finalist 1981; Jameson International finalist 1982

David Taylor, whose white hair earned him the nickname of the 'Silver Fox', was World Amateur Champion in 1968, when he turned professional. He maintained a good ranking without winning a major tournament, but in 1986–87 slipped out of the top 16.

Dennis Taylor

Born: 19 January 1949, N. Ireland
Professional: 1971
Ranking, 1983–87: 13, 11, 4, 3, 8
Best Performances: Embassy World Professional Champion 1985, finalist 1979; Rothmans Grand Prix Champion 1984; Benson and Hedges Masters Champion 1987

Dennis Taylor, for 13 years a man who could not win a major tournament, was rejuvenated in 1983–84 by a new design of spectacles, which enabled him to sight the balls properly for the first time in a long while. With his top 16 ranking threatened, he reached the semi-final of the 1984 World Professional Championship, losing to Steve Davis.

At the beginning of the next season, Dennis was forced to retire from the Jameson when his mother died suddenly. Persuaded by his family to return to the circuit for the Rothmans Grand Prix, he won his first ever major in a very emotional tournament. There was a little reaction after that, but by the time of the 1985 World Championship he was in terrific form again, and his fightback from 0-8 in the final to beat Steve Davis 18-17 on the last black has become a snooker legend. After that, his 1985–86 season was disappointing, but he returned to the top with a Benson and Hedges Masters win in 1986–87.

On becoming World Champion Taylor joined Barry Hearn and is now financially secure. He performs a wonderful comedy exhibition routine, and is a very popular player on the circuit.

Below left: The concentrated delight of Dennis Taylor is obvious in this famous World Championship gesture – the black has just gone into the pocket.

Below: Dennis Taylor, one of the game's great humourists and entertainers, about to perform one of the trick shots which entranced television viewers during a break in World Championship play.

Opposite top: John Spencer, an elegant three times World Champion whose eyesight let him down in the 1980s, but who still shows glimpses of his old masterful form.

Opposite bottom: Kirk Stevens is an exciting player to watch, but has never managed to win a major tournament, although reaching No. 4 in the rankings.

Cliff Thorburn

Born: 16 January 1948, Canada
Professional: 1973
Ranking, 1983–87: 3, 3, 2, 2, 4
Best Performances: Embassy World Professional Champion 1980, finalist 1977, 1983; Benson and Hedges Masters Champion 1983, 1985, 1986; Langs Scottish Masters Champion 1985, 1986; Goya Matchroom Trophy Champion 1985

Below right: Cliff Thorburn, the world No. 4, with the Goya Matchroom trophy he won from the Matchroom professionals in 1985.

Below: Thorburn drives. It looks as if he finds the result funny, but in fact he is a good player who for 147 might even go round twice.

Cliff Thorburn's career is one of the most interesting of the snooker players. In Canada, he played money matches before being inspired by a visit by World Champion John Spencer (whom he played) to try his luck on the British Circuit. After a period of adjustment to the completely different conditions, he won the World Championship in 1980, beating Alex Higgins. His refusal to be beaten earned him the nickname 'The Grinder' and, over the years, he has proved the most difficult player to beat on the circuit. He delights in long matches and late night finishes, has won many important final frames, and has recovered from impossible situations.

Thorburn's biggest moment, outside his world title win, was the 147 maximum break he made in the World Championship of 1983 – the only maximum the championships have seen.

Cliff tried to live in Britain in 1981, but, despite being a World Champion with film-star looks, was not rapturously received, and he returned home to Canada. He came back in 1987 for another try. He has remained in the world's top four longer than any other player, and for a man who prefers golf, that's not bad.

Willie Thorne

Born: 4 March 1954, England
Professional: 1975
Ranking, 1983–87: 18, 12, 11, 7, 11
Best Performances: Mercantile Credit Classic Champion 1985; Matchroom Professional Champion 1986; Langs Scottish Masters finalist 1985; Coral UK Open finalist 1985; Dulux British Open finalist 1986; Benson and Hedges Irish Masters finalist 1986

Willie Thorne had long been acknowledged as the game's best break-builder before he won his first major tournament in 1985. Despite being the master of the

practice table and a large number of 147 breaks, he could not translate this mastery into a sustained run in a tournament. His Mercantile Credit Classic success in 1985, when he beat Davis and Thorburn, gave him more confidence. However, he was still inclined to lose matches to players ranked well below him, and he lost a long lead in the 1985 Coral UK final through casualness. Yet Thorne is now a possible winner of any tournament. In 1986 he joined the Hearn Matchroom squad.

John Virgo

Born: 3 April 1946, England
Professional: 1976
Ranking, 1983–87: 14, 18, 19, 19, 19
Best Performance: Coral UK Champion 1979

John Virgo has won only one major tournament, and has not done justice to his talents in the big televised events. He won the Professional Snooker League in 1984, but the league was soon after wound up with heavy debts. Virgo is a member of the WPBSA board, is occasionally a BBC television snooker commentator, and has a very funny act of impressions of the top players, but he would swop all this for a few victories.

Bill Werbeniuk

Born: 14 January 1947, Canada
Professional: 1973
Ranking, 1983–87: 8, 14, 17, 24, 33
Best Performance: Lada Classic finalist 1983

Bill Werbeniuk's biggest claim to snooker fame derives from the fact that, for a while, the Inland Revenue said that his lager was tax deductible. He drank some 20 pints a day to overcome a nervous disorder which caused his arm to shake. One of the characters of the circuit, which he covered in his caravan, Bill got up to around 20 stone (127 kg). An excellent season in 1982–83, when he was in the Canadian team which won the World Cup, took him to eighth in the rankings, but he has struggled since.

Above: Willie Thorne with the Matchroom Professional trophy he won in 1986. His form is erratic at times, but when in touch there is no smoother player around the table.

Left: John Virgo, one of the game's great entertainers, whose impersonations of other players have delighted live and television audiences alike. This is his view of Dennis Taylor groping for the table.

Jimmy White behind the scenes. He is one of the most popular of modern players, and exciting to watch. Unfortunately his winning frames tend not to last very long.

Barry West

Born: 24 October 1958, England
Professional: 1985
Ranking, 1983–87: —, —, —, 30, 29

In his first season, 1985–86, Barry West reached the quarter-finals of the Coral UK Open, which helped him to his ranking of 30th.

Jimmy White

Born: 2 May 1962, England
Professional: 1980
Ranking, 1983–87: 11, 7, 7, 5, 2
Best Performances: Embassy World Professional finalist 1984, semi-finalist 1982, 1987; Langs Scottish Masters Champion 1981; Benson and Hedges Masters Champion 1984; Benson and Hedges Irish Masters Champion 1985, 1986; Mercantile Credit Classic Champion 1986; Rothmans Grand Prix Champion 1986

Jimmy White is, or was, one of snooker's most precocious talents. He remains the youngest ever English and World Amateur champion, and the youngest winner of a professional tournament (the Langs Scottish Masters when he was aged 19). He was only just 22 when he lost the World Professional Championship 16-14 to Steve Davis in 1984.

White is the smoothest potter in the game, sinking pots from all angles and distances without seeming to line them up. He plays left-handed and very fast, even faster than the 'Hurricane', hence his nickname, the 'Whirlwind'.

White soon added to his initial success, and his habit of making the highest break of a tournament, and at great speed, has made him a big attraction with the public. He appears nerveless, and seems certain to be World Champion one day.

Unfortunately, like his idol Higgins, he has tended to lead a fast life, and has been in trouble for wrecking a hotel room. Although such behaviour was contrary to the image of the Barry Hearn Matchroom, and Hearn was quoted as saying that White would not be part of his team, Jimmy did sign for him in 1986. However, his behaviour at the table is impeccable, and no player calls fouls against himself quicker than Jimmy.

Rex Williams

Born: 20 July 1933, England
Professional: 1951
Ranking, 1983–87: 30, 31, 27, 16, 12
Best Performances: World Professional semi-finalist 1969, 1972, 1974; Rothmans Grand Prix finalist 1986

Rex Williams first challenged for the World Professional Championship in 1965 – 21 years later he produced his best result by reaching the final of the Rothmans Grand Prix, beating Higgins and Steve Davis. He has also been World Billiards Champion. He is chairman of the WPBSA and worked hard to keep snooker going during the slump of the 1950s and 1960s. During the 1987 Embassy World Championship, he was at the centre of the beta-blocker drugs controversy, being an admitted user for medical reasons.

Above: A player whose daredevil shots please the crowd but do not pay in terms of results, where discretion is better rewarded, Cliff Wilson nevertheless does extremely well for a man with practically only one eye.

Cliff Wilson

Born: 10 May 1934, Wales
Professional: 1979
Ranking, 1983–87: 20, 23, 22, 23, 17

In a newspaper article in 1987, Cliff Wilson claimed that modern players do not enjoy the game enough. He clearly relishes it though, playing all games as if he were in the back room of his local club, going for his shots and enjoying a joke. Cliff was a great amateur rival of Ray Reardon, with both being born in Tredegar, Wales. He gave up the game for years, coming back when the money flooded in. He has very poor eyesight (virtually playing with just one eye), and brings a welcome touch of devil-may-care to the circuit.

Left: Rex Williams often appears to have the world against him, and plays with the gravity of an elder statesman, which perhaps is fitting for the chairman of the professionals' ruling body.

Jim Wych

Born: 11 January 1955, Canada
Professional: 1979
Ranking, 1983–87: 43, 41, 52, 32, 36

Jim Wych reached the quarter-final of the World Professional Championship in 1980, his first attempt. He rarely competed on the circuit before 1985–86, when he did enough to earn 32nd place in the world rankings.

BEHIND THE SCENES

Snooker is ruled by a number of bodies. The Billiards and Snooker Control Council (originally formed in 1885 as the Billiards Association) is described as the world governing body for games played on an English billiards table. However, in 1971 the professional game split from the BSCC, whose main function is now to look after the rules for which the Council owns the copyright. The Council keeps records and organizes the English amateur game.

In 1971 the World Billiards and Snooker Council was formed to give overseas national associations more say in the running of the game internationally. Its name was changed in 1973 to the International Billiards and Snooker Federation. The BSCC remains the governing body, but the IBSF controls the World Amateur Championships. The chairman and secretary of the BSCC have similar positions on the IBSF, and the two bodies are complementary.

The professional game is organized by the World Professional Billiards and Snooker Association, which came into being in 1968, arising out of the Professional Billiards Players Association. All professional players are members of the WPBSA, which also has non-playing members and officers. In 1983 the WPBSA (now a limited company) formed a subsidiary, WPBSA Promotions Ltd., to promote professional tournaments. Since the WPBSA decided to

Ray Reardon in his great days as a player. He is now, if not quite the same player, a respected president of the WPBSA.

hold all television contracts for major events, vast sums of money pass through its hands. The Association sponsored the Professional Players Tournament (now replaced by the Rothmans Grand Prix), and now sponsors national professional and amateur championships.

Prominant officers and board members of the WPBSA include: Rex Williams, who was instrumental in its formation, and who has been chairman – apart from the odd period of dispute – ever since; Ray Reardon, six times World Champion, who is president; John Spencer, another ex-World Champion, who is vice-president; Del Simmons, who as a full-time employee is responsible for negotiating all the contracts with television and sponsors; Barry Hearn, Steve Davis' manager, who is on the board of directors; Paul Hatherell, the managing director of WPBSA Promotions Ltd., who came from Embassy, the World Championship sponsors, to become an unofficial spokesman for the board; John Virgo, vice-chairman, David Taylor and Mark Wildman (all of whom are players) and Gordon Ingham, a Yorkshire business man.

The snooker boom has been managed by the WPBSA rather well, but there have been areas of conflict, notably in the fields of contracts and discipline. *Snooker Scene*, the leading magazine of the game, pinpointed problems with contracts procedure in 1986. The success of Hearn, a WPBSA board member, in making contracts for the players he manages and in promoting the game so successfully in many parts of the world, especially the Far East, conflicted with the WPBSA's arrangements in 1987, forcing them to cancel the Belgian Classic. In this instance Hearn's Matchroom players were committed to his new Rothmans Matchroom League, so depriving the Belgian tournament (and an expected large television audience) of its star players.

The criticism of the disciplinary record of the WPBSA is based on an impression that the Association seems, at times, to be more concerned with the hushing up of incidents rather than dealing with them justly. In addition, there is a feeling that an Association whose board contains a majority of current players is the wrong body to mete out punishment to other players, especially when the punishment involves the loss of ranking points, which could indirectly benefit those passing judgement. And, as offences became more serious, and players were obliged to resort to legal representation, there arose the question of whether funds which belonged to all the members should be used to 'prosecute' an accused player (who is himself a member), while he must use private funds to defend himself.

John Spencer, who with Reardon ruled much of the 1970s, watching Higgins in play. Spencer is now vice-president of the WPBSA, and Higgins one of its best customers for disciplinary measures.

Above: Steve Davis, ranked No. 1 in 1986–87, with Neal Foulds, the player moving most rapidly up the rankings, before the 1986 Tennents UK Open final.

Right: Cliff Thorburn, who has maintained a place in the top four of the rankings since his 1980 World Championship victory.

The world ranking list

This list is used to determine the seedings for each tournament, and to exempt the top players from the early rounds. Originally, it was based exclusively on the World Professional Championship results, but it became clear that a player who suffered an early defeat in this one championship, but who was otherwise very successful, would be unfairly affected, even though the rankings were based on results over the last three seasons.

The ranking system was gradually changed until it came to be based on six open tournaments. One was the World Championship, in which points were awarded as follows – ten for the winner, eight to the losing finalist, six to the losing semi-finalists, four to the losers in the last eight, and two to losers in the last 16. The other five tournaments carried half this total of points (i.e. 5, 4, 3, 2, 1).

However, in 1986–87 the system of basing the ranking on three seasons' results was dropped, on the grounds that recent performances should count more than older ones. The ranking list is now based on the results of two seasons only.

The six tournaments in 1985–86 which carried ranking points were the Goya Matchroom Trophy (the BCE International from 1986–87), Rothmans Grand Prix, Coral UK Open (Tennents UK Open from 1986–87), Mercantile Credit Classic, Dulux British Open and the Embassy World Professional Championship (carrying extra points). Extra weight was given to the 1985–86 results by giving points to players who reached the last 32 in a ranking tournament. Thus, the points for the World Championship were 10, 8, 6, 4, 2, 1, and for the other events 6, 5, 4, 3, 2, 1.

Tournaments are seeded as follows – the holder of the title is seeded No. 1, the World Champion (if he is not the title-holder) No. 2, and so on.

Players seeded Nos. 1–16 are exempt until the last 32 of the World Championship, while in the other five events players seeded 1–32 are exempt until the last 64. As the last 64 in these events are guaranteed prize money, players seeded 1–32, and more so those from 1–16, win a few thousand pounds even if they do not win a frame all season.

Snooker referees Jim Thorpe, John Smyth, John Williams, Peter Koniotes and Len Ganley. John Street, the 1986 World Championship final referee, is the best-known of the rest.

Referees

The top referees get more television exposure than the players since they are never eliminated from a tournament, and they have become almost as familiar. The senior referee is Welshman John Williams, who has officiated in five World Championship finals. He was a civil servant who took up refereeing full time when his job was lost in public sector economies.

John Smyth was the first to become a full-time professional referee, having worked for London Transport on the underground system. He has been involved in more controversies than most, including the well-publicized occasion when he failed to hear Cliff Thorburn nominate a green, and penalized him seven points. He also upset Ray Reardon over a touching ball incident, after which the outspoken Reardon suggested he should get some spectacles, advice which John Smyth took, to his own advantage.

Len Ganley, like Smyth an Irishman, has become well-known as the 'ballcrusher' following his part in a lager television advertisement, in which he crushes a snooker ball in his fist. Ganley is nearly 20 stone (127 kg), and gives the impression of being not one to argue with over a decision.

John Street, from Devon, who refereed the 1986 World Championship final won by Joe Johnson, only became a full-time referee in 1985. Previously he sold insurance, where his television exposure proved an asset, but like the others he has no regrets at refereeing full-time.

Jim Thorpe, from Salford, still works as a representative for a carpet company. His most publicized controversy concerns a push shot in a match between Dennis Taylor and Kirk Stevens, which resulted in his being taken off the match. However, he was soon back keeping the players in the best of order.

Above: The BBC team of commentators, whose voices, particularly around the end of April, are among the best known in the land. From the left: Jack Karnehm, Willie Thorne, presenter David Vine, Clive Everton, John Virgo and 'Whispering' Ted Lowe. Thorne and Virgo are still hoping to lift that trophy.

Right: Clive Everton in the television commentary box at the Crucible. The commentators have a very good view of the World Championship play.

Television presenters

The number of commentators employed by the television channels to describe the snooker tournaments has risen with the hours devoted to the game, and there are enough of them now to put on a substitute tournament if none of the players turned up. And some of them are pretty useful, too.

The doyen of the BBC broadcasters is Ted Lowe, whose snooker experience goes back to managing the Leicester Square Hall for Joe Davis after the Second World War. His first commentaries were given before there was a commentary box, hence his hushed tones, which ensure that he does not disturb the players. He has maintained this style, and is known as 'Whispering' Ted Lowe.

Jack Karnehm, a World Amateur Billiards Champion, is a national coach. He had much to do with Dennis Taylor's switch to the large new glasses which brought him such success. Jack's most famous words came while he was doing the commentary when Cliff Thorburn made his 147 break, worth £10,000; his 'Good luck, mate' as Cliff neared the end, spoke for the nation.

Jim Meadowcroft, who played much of his teenage snooker with Dennis Taylor and Alex Higgins, is the only one of the three who did not become World Champion. He did not quite make the top (he was ranked No.85 in 1986–87), but is very busy on the holiday camp circuit as resident professional when he is not broadcasting.

Clive Everton is another player (ranked 100 in 1986–87), but his main connection with the sport is as a writer. He edits *Snooker Scene*, owns *Cue World*, is the *Guardian* correspondent, and has had a hand in many snooker books, including the original *Guinness Book of Snooker* and *The History of Snooker and Billiards*.

Independent Television uses a number of players as commentators. Like Karnehm and Everton, they are great billiards players. Rex Williams, a former World Billiards Champion, is on the team, though as he is ranked 16 in the world he is occasionally unavailable, being on the table himself.

Mark Wildman also has a respectable ranking (43) and he, too, is a former World Billiards Champion. At one time he left the game for a spell in banking, but now combines his twin expertise nicely for, besides being a good talker, he is also a good judge when it comes to a financial speculation on the result.

Ray Edmonds is also an ex-Billiards World Champion (are billiards players better talkers than snooker players?) He combines his broadcasting with a snooker equipment business and a club at Grimsby, the home town of Mike Hallett and Dean Reynolds.

Further commentaries come from John Pulman, an ex-World Champion snooker player, Dennis Taylor, John Spencer and John Virgo, while ITV are fond of calling on their horse-racing betting expert, John McCririck, to relay the latest betting in his eccentric manner.

The BBC and ITV networked 373 hours of snooker in the 1985–86 season.

John Pulman, World Champion of the 1960s and now a distinctive voice on ITV transmissions of snooker tournaments.

Mike Watterson in play in the UK Championships. Watterson, a snooker and soccer entrepreneur, was involved with many of the leading tournaments, including the World Championship and the World Cup.

Hearn's Matchroom professionals – the 'winning team' as he advertises them – in 1986-87. From left: Willie Thorne, Jimmy White, Neal Foulds, Dennis Taylor, Hearn, Tony Meo, Terry Griffiths and Steve Davis.

Managers and promoters

One of the promoters who put snooker on its way to boom-time is Mike Watterson, who promoted the World Championship at the Crucible Theatre, Sheffield, in 1977. When Embassy moved in to sponsor it, Watterson could claim to have put together two of the elements which make the annual television festival such a success.

Watterson (no mean player, being ranked 77 in 1986–87) successfully promoted other tournaments and held contracts with BBC and ITV. But it was his success that probably led to his downfall.

Eventually, the WPBSA, who by controlling the players virtually control the tournaments, decided to promote the tournaments themselves and engaged Watterson's assistant, Paul Hatherell, to run their promotions company. As Watterson's contracts expired, the WPBSA took them over.

The snooker boom naturally attracted managers and agents, the most successful being Barry Hearn. As a chartered accountant dealing in property speculation, his company purchased 17 Lucania Snooker Halls in 1974. In 1976 he spotted Steve Davis in one of them. He went into snooker management with Davis, Geoff Foulds (father of Neal) and Vic Harris as his first signings. Then he sold 16 of his 17 halls to Riley Leisure (becoming one of its directors) in 1982, but he kept the Romford hall and turned it into the Romford Snooker Centre, which remains his headquarters, the old matchroom being transformed into The Matchroom night club.

In addition to Davis, Hearn's players are Tony Meo, whom he signed in 1981, Terry Griffiths in 1982, Dennis Taylor in 1985 (after he had won the World Championship), and Willie Thorne, Neal Foulds and Jimmy White in 1986.

Hearn keeps a very close eye on his players, even keeping their chequebooks. All they have to do is play, pick up the endorsements and keep the clients happy. As his seven players are all ranked in the top 13, he controls at least half the earning power of all snooker players. His

Barry Hearn and one of his first, and undoubtedly most successful signings, Steve Davis. The trophies kept rolling in.

Joe Johnson, 1986 World Professional Snooker Champion, doing what he likes best, singing with his group 'Made in Japan'.

magnificent seven earned about £820,000 in 1985–86 from tournament winnings alone and approaching the World Championship of 1987 had won all the other five ranking tournaments during the season.

Of course, winnings are a small part of the Matchroom players' scheme. By insisting on a high standard of behaviour from all his players, and an attractive image, he ensures that they are marketable in all sorts of ways. In 1984, for instance, Davis signed a much-publicized contract with Courage, the brewers, who, in return for his services for 40 days a year, made him an instant millionaire.

Hearn is now so powerful that he can promote his own tournaments. In 1986, while Thorburn retained his Langs Scottish Masters, the traditional opener to the snooker season worth £13,000 to the winner, Willie Thorne was winning Hearn's new Matchroom Trophy, restricted to his own players, pocketing £50,000 for his trouble. Hearn also announced a new Rothmans Matchroom League, with proposals to stage matches all over Europe. He is rapidly becoming as powerful as the WPBSA, of which he is a board member, and clearly is likely to be the most powerful man in the game in the future.

The best player not in the Matchroom stable is Cliff Thorburn (whose manager is another millionaire, Robert Winsor). Nonetheless, he has been included in the initial Rothmans League, being the only player not under Hearn's management. Thorburn also accompanied the Matchroom tour of the Far East in the summer of 1986. Also with Robert Winsor are Jim Wych and Dene O'Kane and, from 1987, Kirk Stevens.

The one remaining powerful management group is Howard Kruger's Framework Management and Agency, which represents Alex Higgins, Joe Johnson, Tony Knowles, John Parrott and Eugene Hughes.

An interesting diversion from snooker rankings occurred in 1986 when the Hearn squad, which did not then include Neal Foulds or Jimmy White, teamed up with Cockney songsters Chas and Dave to record the pop song *Snooker Loopy*. The clean-cut Hearn boys were challenged by the Framework 'mob' of bad boys, which at the time consisted of White, Tony Knowles and Alex Higgins, who with guest 'star' Kirk Stevens, recorded *The Wanderer*, a recent Status Quo revival. Meanwhile, Joe Johnson, the World Champion, recorded with his group, 'Made in Japan', an old number called *Everlasting Love*. The Hearn quintet, or more probably the famous Chas and Dave duo, won, their song reaching No. 5 in the charts, while the others sank without trace.

World Champion Alison Fisher came to the fore in the 1980s and proved to be as good as any of the male amateurs of her age. Perhaps with her, women's snooker will really take off.

Julie Islip (left) and Mandy Fisher, two of the leading women players of the 1980s, played in a television tournament.

Women's Snooker

Competitions for women have lagged behind the men's, and with unlimited demand for the top male players there had been little serious effort to promote this aspect of the game. However, some ladies have been good enough to make their names known, among them Vera Selby, Mandy Fisher, Stacey Hillyard, and Natalie Stelmach. The World Ladies Billiards and Snooker Association (WLBSA), with Gaye Jones as tournament director and Mandy Fisher as secretary, has now begun to campaign forcefully for the women's game, and they have a potential matchwinner in Alison Fisher, a brilliant teenage player who is already not far short of the best male amateurs. She won the 1986 Women's World Championship from 56 entrants at Breaks, Solihull, beating in the final Sue LeMaich, a Canadian who owns her own snooker club in Toronto.

INDEX

Page numbers in *italic* refer to the illustrations